UNGODLY

TERRENCE BROTHERS

A NOVEL

Library of Congress Cataloging-in-Publication Data is available upon request.

Paperback ISBN 978-1-7337303-4-1
Ebook ISBN 978-1-7337303-5-8

Cover design by Arcane Book Covers
Printed in USA

CHAPTER 1

Fabulous Las Vegas, Nevada—also known as the city of lights, the city that never sleeps, and perhaps, its most popular tagline—Sin City. The large metropolis of Nevada has more than two million residents and is notoriously known for attracting millions of tourists each year—gaining the reputation of being the fastest growing city on earth, the wedding capital of the world, and the gambling mecca of the universe.

The most well-known city in the Nevada desert has countless labels, but is it really as spectacular as it's thought to be? Everyone knows that it's a town that was once ruled by the Chicago mob, but also has a long history of catering to a plethora of whales and high-rollers that flock to the casinos, who are perhaps, the only ones who can truly afford to gamble and try their luck. As for the risk-takers who really can't afford to take such risks, since they fail to recognize the odds are stacked against them, unfortunately, they're forced to break the bank and are sent home. But, of course, not all can afford to get home. Some are left stranded and heartbroken, giving the city of Las Vegas the green light to tear them apart.

TERRENCE BROTHERS

The desert city is known for its ruthlessness. It has more cash readily available than the U.S. Treasury, largely built by gangsters and gamblers—heavily relying on the marks who try but fail. *Marks* are the unsuspecting gamblers that the casinos prey upon. The ones who've lost all self-control, placing bet after bet, spinning wheel after wheel, rolling dice after dice, pulling arm after arm on a medley of slot machines, trying to recapture funds they've already lost, just to find themselves deeper and deeper in debt.

The city of dreams and opportunity is filled with a myriad of traps. It entices people of all cultures, from all walks of life, to travel from abroad just to visit a city they'd only seen on T.V.

The glamorous city is guaranteed to supply free alcoholic beverages to every adult who continues to gamble, hoping to boost their libidos or other agendas by surrounding them with provocative, scantily-clad women, whether it be strippers, showgirls, cocktail waitresses, keno runners, or prostitutes, but the moment an unsuspecting visitor barely crosses the line, the casinos personnel are quick to complicate their lives by calling the authorities and having them thrown in jail, instead of detaining them until they sober up then release them to go wherever they please. After all, the casinos are the enablers who contributed to the tourist's predicament—something the city's representatives will never admit to, since swindling out-of-towners out of bail and attorney money is great for the economy—something no one would dare argue against, especially those who experience it firsthand.

UNGODLY

Las Vegas is a city that uses its big beautiful casinos and mega resorts as magnets to attract locals and people from all across the globe. The nice cars, homes, beautiful bright lights, magnificent architecture, amazing landscapes—accentuating the flashy clothes, jewelry and expensive veneer smiles of those who stroll up and down the well-lit streets of the Strip and Downtown, could all possibly be a facade, after all, the city wasn't coined Sin City for nothing…

It's almost certain that anyone who's ever been to Las Vegas can easily come up with a few ideas of their own about why a city so glamorous and wonderfully exciting was once said to be taboo, and is still believed to be cursed, but whatever individual opinions are, whatever anyone thinks the risks and dangers are, everyone has the same thing in common—they all seek to experience the American Dream. Everyone wants to win a fortune, so they flock to Las Vegas to try their luck.

The city welcomes millions and millions of visitors each year with open arms, but the wonderful city hasn't always been this way.

The city of Las Vegas has a lot of secrets.

One of its biggest secrets is that it hasn't always been receptive to African-Americans, and no one knew this better than sixty-two-year-old Buddy Armstrong—the founder and pastor of Real Love Baptist Church. He and his extremely adorable sixty-year-old wife Willa Armstrong—better known as Sister Willa, were lifelong residents of West Las Vegas. They lived on Madison Avenue, only a few blocks away from the church they built.

The Christian couple managed to stay married for over thirty-five years but decided early on in their relationship that they had no desires to bear any children. Partly because they were both young and wild at that time in their lives—the other reason was because of the way minorities were treated.

It was the awful time in Las Vegas' history when African-Americans weren't allowed in the so-called white parts of town, especially not after nightfall—they were only permitted to reside and socialize on the west side. Particularly in a neighborhood known as Berkely Square, the first housing development blacks were allowed to live, on the corner of D Street and Lake Mead Boulevard.

The west side was basically a plantation for blacks, although many were too ashamed or uneducated to view it that way.

The disadvantaged race of people was faced with circumstances of which they had no control, so accepting it and making the necessary adjustments became automatic for them, but those were the ones who wanted to survive.

Accepting conditions that were clearly unacceptable and inhumane was a part of everyday life, it was all part of what was known as the black experience.

Being limited and restricted from the so-called better things in life was nothing new to the blacks who were around in that era, so they mastered making the best out of whatever they had. They realized they hadn't asked for West Las Vegas—West Las Vegas was given to them.

UNGODLY

It was forced on them and labeled their side of town, so they made their side of town the best place to be by building and opening up black-owned and operated businesses and watched them flourish expeditiously.

With so many hurdles, obstacles, roadblocks and bloodshed along its path, it was quite obvious to everyone within the black community that the adversary intended to watch them fail. They refused to succumb to failure and ostracism. Instead, they set out to do some amazing things.

Although more than a few perished, it was actually a beautiful and distinct time in American history when black folks actually believed in and supported each other—something that seems to be a rarity in this day and age.

Miraculously, the pastor and his wife remained close back in the day when Jesus Christ wasn't anywhere in their lives—when their relationship consisted only of sexual trysts and sin—the favorite part of their day being the Vegas nightlife.

They frequented such establishments as the historic Moulin Rouge, Love's Cocktail Lounge, The Colony Club, Sugar Hill, The People's Choice, Chances 'R', The Town Tavern, The Brown Derby, The West Side Story, Seven Seas, Elk's Lounge and, the V.F.W. Post.

The Armstrongs often rented a room at a small casino in the heart of the west side on Jackson Street known as the Cove, that was also once occupied by the late greats Sammie Davis Jr. and R&B sensation Natalie Cole.

Willa and Buddy's sexcapades developed into something much more serious once they realized they had fallen in love…

Things in Las Vegas were a lot different in those days—the city has since evolved one hundred and eighty degrees—it's now become one of the most diverse cities in the nation—blacks can now go wherever they please.

Willa Armstrong stood with one hand propped on her curvaceous hip while her well-endowed backside pressed against the dresser. "I don't like the idea not one bit," she said as she rolled her eyes, infuriated that her husband was avoiding eye contact. "There's something about it that doesn't sit well with me."

They had just gotten a visit from an old acquaintance named Lisa Miles—a drug addicted woman they once ran the streets with, who had a seventeen-year-old daughter she could no longer control.

There was a time when the Armstrongs used to drink alcohol, smoke marijuana, angel dust, and snort cocaine with Lisa on a daily basis—an activity they had long stopped indulging in since giving their life to Christ, but Lisa refused to stop self-destructing and acted as though she didn't want to shake the habit of smoking crack cocaine.

The Armstrongs could only stare in awe as their old acquaintance broke down in tears, explaining to them how impossible it had become to look after her daughter, who seemed to have lost all respect for the woman who had given her life—she apparently felt like she didn't have a mother, something she often said when she was upset.

Pastor Armstrong agreed to take her in. He knew from being around the rambunctious teen in the past that she was very intelligent and full of potential, so instead of allowing her to end up in a shelter or out on the streets as her mom suggested, he felt it was his duty as a pastor and a neighborhood leader to provide the teen with a loving home. The problem was, he took it upon himself and made the decision without first checking to see if it was okay with his wife. It wasn't long before he realized he'd made a mistake.

He told Lisa to have her daughter at the church at two o'clock the following day after being informed she was good at math. It piqued his interest to learn that the out-of-control teen loved working with numbers— his plan was to present her with a job offer.

Lisa Miles was ecstatic when she heard the news.

Pastor Armstrong could still visualize her excitement when she left his house, although he knew Lisa was still heavily on drugs, she didn't have the appearance of the average drug user, she was well preserved compared to other addicts he'd seen. Lisa still had the pretty-dimpled smile she was known for although her teeth could use some dentistry, he thought. Her face was the complexion of smooth almond butter and her long jet-black hair was pulled tight in a bun. The tan yoga pants she wore clung tightly to her curves, she was well endowed in all the right places, possessing a figure not even the pastor could ignore.

"Buddy, you can't just sit there and act like you don't hear me talking to you," his wife said while staring at him. "We're talking about a young girl who thinks she's grown. She's already proven herself to be very promiscuous, and you're talking about making her part of the clergy? Before you get all gung-ho, you should stop and think about how the rest of the congregation might feel about it."

Pastor Armstrong remained sitting at the foot of their bed, acting as though he was reading scriptures from his Bible, pretending like he was too preoccupied to respond at the moment—one of several bad habits his wife had grown to hate.

The two had worked feverishly together to build a solid reputation that was highly favorable to Real Love Baptist Church—the most prominent church in West Las Vegas, serving a diverse congregation of nearly two thousand members.

"Sweetheart, the Bible orders us not to pass judgment and to accept everyone for who they are," he finally said without looking at her, already knowing she was peering down at him. "Sometimes we have to do what's right in God's eyes, and not worry about what others might think about it."

"I understand you're a great man, Buddy," his wife began. "I also understand that it's your obligation to do God's work, but you've already done a lot of great things for this community and for the members of the church, so we have to be careful who we invite into the House of God, even when we reserve good intentions."

Pastor Armstrong shut his Bible, which appeared to have been read multiple times over. "Willa, I can't believe you're passing judgment on this young child," he said with dismay. "Her upbringing has been very unfortunate. I shouldn't have to remind you that it's not her fault."

"I'm not saying it's her fault, honey, but you can't act like it's yours or mine either," his wife retorted. "It's not our fault Lisa has chosen drugs over her own child. She should never have gotten pregnant if she wasn't prepared to take care of her responsibility. It's her job to care for Erica, not ours. We can't just sit back and let her push her burden on us."

The pastor took a few moments to reflect on his past. He knew it was only by the grace of God that he and Willa were able to escape the streets. The cocaine epidemic had swept through the black community like the plague, destroying thousands of lives in the process. He and his wife had often talked about how blessed they were, so he knew she understood how fortunate they were to have escaped its path, he found it hard to believe she was acting this way. "Baby, I don't want to get into pointing fingers, but we've all made some mistakes in life," he said before continuing. "I truly believe that if it wasn't for God showing us favor, we could both very easily still be in the streets. We were once just like Lisa, remember? We can't look down on her now just because we've cleaned up."

Willa's eyes looked like daggers as she stared at her husband, she couldn't believe he'd said such a thing. "You don't think I already know that?" she said as she moved toward him, waiving her finger in the air while awaiting an answer. "You don't need to remind me of something like that! By no means am I saying we're better than her. I know darn well I've made my share of mistakes, but what does that have to do with us coming to the rescue and taking care of a child Lisa gave birth to? It's not our fault the child turned out to be as bad as she is."

"Young Erica is just a product of the environment she grew up in," her husband replied mildly. "She's an innocent victim just like so many of our black youth. Black folks haven't always been given options. Most times we didn't have a choice, so we accepted whatever white folks were willing to give us, and most of the time they weren't willing to give us anything."

"Lisa doesn't have to keep participating in getting high, Buddy. She does it because she wants to," Willa said in a softer tone. "She had the opportunity to get out of the streets the same time we did, but since she still chooses to keep going down the same destructive path, I think we should make her suffer the consequences."

"This is about Erica, not Lisa," her husband told her.

"Regardless of the bad choices her mom made, that girl is old enough to know right from wrong, it ain't no sense in us feeling sorry for her," the older woman said without blinking an eye. "She made a choice just like her mom to be out of control, we shouldn't be the ones taking responsibility for her."

"She's only doing what she knows," Pastor Armstrong said in the young girl's defense. "Her mom was not there like she should have been, so it's up to good people like you and I to intervene and do what we know is right. We have to devote some of our time to teach her what's right, and not be so quick to pass judgment on her."

"I'm not passing judgment," his wife told him. "I'm just trying to look out for the best interest of the congregation—the very people who make it possible for you and I to eat."

"That's understandable, sweetheart, there's nothing wrong with it," her husband said in a deep voice. "We should never pass judgment on anyone. We should try our best to accept people for who they are and appreciate them while they're still with us. We have to be careful when dealing with strangers, because we never know when we're in the presence of an angel."

"How in the world can Erica Miles be compared to an angel?" Sister Willa inquired, feeling as though he'd given a bad example.

"I'm not comparing them," her husband said. "I'm just saying we shouldn't speak ill of anyone. Whether you realize it or not, honey, you calling Erica promiscuous is passing judgment on her."

"I just don't want to have to deal with her," his wife said, truthfully.

Pastor Armstrong looked at the floor and began speaking while nodding his head. "That poor child has never had a father," he said sympathetically. "I've never understood how a man can so easily turn his back on his own children as if they're not even a part of him. To me, that's just like turning your back on your own self—God knows it's something I could never do. It's a true blessing to be able to see tiny replicas of yourself, but so many men don't appreciate it, nor do they deserve it."

Sister Willa realized it was a lost cause trying to plead with her husband. She started walking toward the bedroom door but didn't leave the room before cleverly sliding in her final remark. "I don't give a damn what she's been through! She's not our child or our responsibility. You shouldn't have agreed to take her in without my consent," she said before disappearing into the hallway, leaving her husband by his lonesome to wallow in guilt.

Pastor Armstrong considered retracting his invitation, but because he had already given Lisa his word, no matter how bad he began to feel or what his wife thought, he knew he had to stay strong and stick to his guns.

CHAPTER 2

Hesitation was obvious as Erica Miles stepped over the threshold of Real Love Baptist Church, not remembering the last time she attended services, but since she still believed in God to some degree, she immediately sensed that her spandex skirt was inappropriate. *Oh well* she thought as the large decorative glass door shut softly behind her.

She tiptoed through the lobby, entered the main part of the church before stopping in the back to look around. "Hello," she said aloud after not seeing anyone, receiving her own echo as her only feedback. Erica began to wonder if her mom had lied, something she'd done several times in the past, but she was secretly hoping it wasn't the case this time. The young teen had never seen the church empty before, she was taken aback by its enormous size.

She was amazed by the gold and burgundy décor that was immaculately spread throughout the building—accentuating the pews, the pulpit and the choir stand—complemented by brass-plated chandeliers that hovered aloft. To the teen it looked like a church she'd seen on T.V., making her wonder how much money had been spent putting it together.

She continued to gaze around as she moved forward, feeling extremely small inside the massive building. She walked briskly up the aisle, not having an inkling where she was going or which direction to head, up until this point, she hadn't even considered where she was supposed to meet him.

The mere silence made her think that she was alone, so she became more at ease with each step she took, suddenly wanting to know what it felt like to stand behind the pulpit.

"Hey, ma," a voice said from afar, causing the seventeen-year-old to stop dead in her tracks. Erica looked around slowly but didn't see anyone until something instinctively told her to look up.

"Who you're lookin' for, ma?" a woman said from the balcony as soon as she and Erica made eye contact.

Erica stared at the woman who was obviously a janitor. She could see that she was beautiful, even from a distance, appearing to be somewhere in her early to mid-thirties. "I'm looking for Pastor Armstrong," Erica responded, suddenly hoping her job offer wouldn't be cleaning the church. "He told me to be here at 2 o'clock today, but I have no idea where I'm supposed to meet him."

The woman pointed to a door to the left of the choir stand, about sixty feet away from where Erica was standing. "He's in his office. I'm sure he's probably waiting for you."

"Thank you," Erica said as she walked toward the door, popping her chewing gum loudly as if she was at home.

A short hallway appeared when she went through the door, and after bending a corner, she saw the door ajar to Pastor Armstrong's office— he was sitting at his desk, reading his Bible.

"Well hello, young lady—good afternoon," he said with vigor as he flipped the Bible shut, extending his hand.

Seeing Pastor Armstrong reminded Erica of a neighbor who once lived in the apartment next door to her mother—everyone knew him as Old Man Charlie, but as far as she knew, she was the only one in the neighborhood who called him daddy. Old Man Charlie had given her the nickname Sticky-Kat, because she'd let him eat candy, fruit and other sweet treats from her vagina when she was fourteen and fifteen years old—something he just couldn't get enough of. She was sad when the old man suddenly died from an apparent heart attack—a reaction her mom and other neighbors struggled to understand, because everyone had the impression that she couldn't stand him. It was exactly what she and Charlie wanted everyone to think, it's how they kept their rendezvous from being detected.

Old Man Charlie passed away eighteen months prior. Every older man she encountered reminded her of him. "Good afternoon," she said humbly while eyeing the pastor, wondering if he and Old Man Charlie had anything in common. "My mom said you wanted me to come see you today."

"Yep, I told her to send you," Pastor Armstrong said before leaning back in his chair. "Your mom said she's been having a lot of problems with you lately. Tell me what's going on if you don't mind."

"My mom be trippin'," Erica said nonchalantly as she sat down, making sure to lean forward to showcase her cleavage.

"In what way?"

"In every way," she said with emphasis. "She act like she don't want me to grow up or something; she got something to say about everything I do."

"You growing up is inevitable," Pastor Armstrong said in a caring voice, fighting hard to keep control of his wandering eye. "I'm sure your mom knows that she can't control the forces of nature, so explain to me what you mean by that."

"She just be trippin'," the teen repeated. "She trips about every little thing I do as if she didn't do the same things when she was my age."

"Things like what, Erica?" he said, concerned. "It's okay to be specific. There's no need to keep beating around the bush."

"I'm young and I like having fun, so I might drink a lil bit…smoke a lil weed…have sex sometimes…you know, the same things all young adults do," she said coyly.

Pastor Armstrong sighed, slumped his shoulders and started scratching his head before speaking. "You're too young to be doing any of those things, Erica, so I think I may have to side with your mom on this one."

Ahh shit, another goody-two-shoes Erica thought to herself but decided to go ahead and respond to what she construed as his opinion. "Well, apparently, we do things in my generation that y'all didn't do in y'alls. But if that's the case, where did my generation come from?"

Pastor Armstrong decided to change the subject. He didn't have time to sit and argue with a seventeen-year-old, so he knew it was best to move forward. "Did your mom tell you she's putting you out?"

"She always say stupid shit like that," Erica said bluntly, not caring that she was sitting inside a church. "She just be talkin' out the side of her neck, bitchin' at me 'cause she's going through something."

Pastor Armstrong was uncomfortable with her choice of words. It was his first glimpse at what Lisa had talked about. "Watch your mouth, young lady. Let's not forget this is the House of God," he warned but didn't reveal how offended he really was. "You have to be mindful to give the Lord his due. I hope to never hear you talk like that again."

"I'm sorry," she said giggling, seeming to think everything he said was a joke. "Did she tell you she wants me to leave?"

"Yes, and I think she's serious this time," he said calmly. "She was ready to throw you out on the street or send you to a shelter, so my wife and I told her we'll take you in," Pastor Armstrong said, knowing what he said was only partially true. He figured if he told her the whole truth, he would have potentially opened the door for her to reject his offer, which would have defeated the purpose of the entire meeting.

"Take me in for what—I'm almost grown?" Erica said as she arched her eyebrows, watching his eyes to see if he was checking her out.

"Almost doesn't cut it. You're not there yet," the pastor retorted as he pulled a tissue from his pocket and blew his nose.

Erica crossed her legs, gave it some thought before words slowly began to spiel from her lips. "I guess I'll go ahead and move in with you and your wife for now," she said with reluctance in her voice. "I'll be eighteen in five months, then I'll legally be able to do whatever I want."

"Until then, you're going to have to abide by our rules, is that understood?"

"Yeah, I guess," Erica said, slightly rolling her eyes. "And, what is it you'd like me to do, pastor?"

"You can start by removing that thing from your mouth, whatever it is you keep putting between your teeth," he said while pointing his finger, using the opportunity to gaze at the fullness of her lips.

"Oh, my tongue ring?" she said blushing. "It would definitely be a first if you're saying you don't like my tongue ring, because most men think it's sexy as hell."

"I'm not one of those men, so please remove it whenever time permits," he said sternly, already regretting his decision to be a good samaritan. He knew that he had more than likely bitten off more than he could chew, so he said a quick prayer, asking the Lord for strength.

The teen had a lot of experience when it came to dealing with men and had already formed the opinion that men were easy. Despite Pastor Armstrong being a man of God, she felt as long as he was still of the human species, she would have him eating out the palm of her hand in no time. She decided to work on him slowly but surely. "So, does that mean I have to remove my nipple, naval and clit rings, too?"

"Young lady, let's get one thing straight," he said as he stood up. "I'm not your boyfriend or some Joe Blow from the streets who wants to flirt with you. I am a man who believes in God, and I try my best to do right by him. That's the only reason I agreed to do your mom this favor. Let me know if I made a mistake by agreeing to help, because it's not too late for me to change my mind."

Erica began to feel guilty about her naughty behavior. She could sense the sincerity in the pastor's voice—she had never heard a man speak with so much passion. "No," she said before continuing. "Forgive me if I offended you, Pastor Armstrong. I'm just not used to someone caring about me."

"Young lady, your mother has always cared about you," the pastor assured her. "She probably hasn't always known how to show you, but I personally know that she's always cared."

"Yeah, I know she did," said Erica. "She just cared about dope and getting high a lot more."

Pastor Armstrong couldn't refute what the teen had said, so he took it for what it was and moved on. "Well, let's not be too harsh on her, because I'm sure we've all made our share of mistakes," he said before continuing. "Your room at my house is already set up for you. We can get you moved in today if that's okay with you?"

"It's fine with me, but what's this about you're supposed to be giving me a job?"

"That's right, I almost forgot about that," he said before pausing. "I do have a job for you, but that's only if you don't mind working here at the church. I can only afford to pay you minimum wage."

"Don't tell me you want me to help clean up?" Erica said as she thought about the overalls-wearing woman she'd seen on the balcony.

"No, what makes you say that?"

"The woman who pointed your office out to me looked like she was cleaning up or something?"

"Danielle," said Pastor Armstrong. "She's my custodian who was once a troubled teen herself. She's the best I know at what she does, so there wouldn't be a need in getting help for her."

"Good," said Erica.

"Yeah, she's a hard worker. I'm sure she has all the cleaning covered."

"So, what is it you need me to do then?"

"I hear you like working with numbers?"

"I do, but what does that have to do with anything?"

"Your job would be to count the weekly offerings and tithes, but that's only if you give me your word that I can trust you."

"You can trust me," she said almost instantly, not really certain if she could trust herself. "Will I have help?"

"Do you need it?"

"I don't know, it all depends."

"On what?"

"I guess on how much time I have and how much I gotta count," the teen said, bashfully.

"It usually takes my wife a day or two to count it and get it logged, but she usually don't work no more than an hour a day," the pastor said. "The job is simple—I'll have her show you what you need to do, and, if necessary, I can always call on her to help you get it done."

"Alright, that's cool. I accept," Erica said in a soft voice. "Am I taking her job?"

"Yeah, kind of, but she'll be okay."

The teen felt a little uneasy about taking the older woman's job, she wondered if she should reconsider accepting the position. "What will she do now that I'm filling this position?"

"Well, all she gotta do now is look pretty," the pastor said humorously.

"Is there anything else I'll need to know?"

"There is," replied Pastor Armstrong, appearing to be ten years younger than he actually was. "In fact, a couple of things."

She batted her eyes and said, "I'm listening."

"Well, bookkeeping is only part of the job—you'll also have to double as my secretary; answer the phone, write down messages, appointments, and tidy up in here when necessary."

"I can handle that," Erica said, smiling. "Is that it?"

"Yeah, that's pretty much it," the pastor told her. "At least for around here, but you'll have some rules to abide by while you're under my roof. No drugs, alcohol, boys or sex, period. Is that understood?"

She pondered a bit and said, "Understood. I don't think I'm as wild or fast as you think I am."

"I don't think you're either of those things," the pastor told her. "I'm not here to pass judgment on you, Erica, but I don't think you always make the best decisions for yourself either."

"Who does?" she said in agreement. "We all do our share of fuckin' up sometimes. Life is about living and learning."

"Add that to our list of rules," he said sternly. "There won't be any profanity in my house or inside the church. We're really going to have to do something about that filthy mouth of yours!"

"Ooops, I'm sorry, Pastor Armstrong. It slipped," she said with a giggle, not taking anything he said too seriously.

"You better not let it slip again."

"I'm not used to being inside nobody's church, and I'm damn sure not used to people opening up their homes and lives to me," she said sincerely. "It's going to take a little getting used to."

"You'll be okay," the pastor told her. "I know I keep bringing up more and more rules, but there's also going to be a dress code of what you can and can't wear," he said while looking at her.

"I already know this outfit isn't going to cut it," she said while peering down at herself, seeing her fully exposed cleavage staring back at her. "I knew I should have worn something different as soon as I walked in here."

"Pay closer attention to what you say, wear, and do, and everything else should take care of itself," the pastor said softly. "You can't be in here or at my house with your breasts and backside hanging all out. My wife is certainly not going to go for that."

"Pastor Armstrong, I know you're an older man, but you're not blind, so you can't expect me to hide what I can't hide, but I'll do my best to stay covered up."

Pastor Armstrong blushed. He knew he couldn't refute what the teen had said—she definitely had a lot to work with. "Go to your mom's place and pack your things. I'll be there shortly to take you home."

The teen paused for a moment after the pastor spoke. She knew he had no idea how special he made her feel, at no time in her life had anyone made her feel so important. "Thanks for caring," she whispered as she climbed to her feet, she was nearly in tears when she left his office.

"How'd it go, ma?" the woman said from the balcony when she spotted Erica, who seemed to be in some kind of hurry.

Erica looked up at her and gave her a thumbs up. She was tempted to stop and chat with the woman the pastor said was Danielle—there was something about the woman that piqued her interest.

She was nearly at a jog when she left the church—she couldn't wait to get from under her mother's roof.

Erica looked around the small guest bedroom at the Armstrong residence, wondering as she unpacked her belongings, if the closet space was big enough to hold all of her clothing. Her keen intuition couldn't help but notice the pair of piercing dark-colored eyes that seemed to penetrate her skull as they zeroed in on her from the bedroom doorway. Pastor Armstrong gave her a heads up about his wife's untrusting nature during the short trip from her mother's apartment, so she was somewhat anticipating the unwanted attention.

Mrs. Armstrong realized her presence had been detected, so she stepped out of the shadows, and into the bedroom. "Hello, Ms. Erica," she said in a warm-welcoming voice.

"Hello," Erica said in a receptive tone, laying clothes across the bed she pulled from the suitcase. She turned to glance at Mrs. Armstrong's attire and was immediately proud of herself for taking the time to tone down her outfit before walking out the door of her mother's apartment. There was no denying the woman's curves underneath her conservative clothing—the teen found herself impressed by the older woman's appearance. Her physique was quite admirable, she hoped she'd still look as good when she reached her age.

"My husband did have a talk with you, right?"

"Yeah, we had *the talk*," Erica said with no enthusiasm, hoping she wasn't about to be hit with another lecture.

"Okay," replied Mrs. Armstrong. "I just wanted to personally welcome you into my home to let you know that we accept you with open arms."

"Thank you," Erica said, surprised. "Hearing you say that means a lot to me." Considering what she'd been told by Pastor Armstrong, Erica didn't expect such a warm welcome from the Christian woman—she immediately began to have second thoughts about her.

"A daughter of Lisa's is a daughter of ours, so we're glad to be able to do her this favor."

"Thank you, Mrs. Armstrong," Erica said as she leaned in to hug her. "You guys have no idea how much this means to me. I hope I'll be able to make you and my mom proud."

"Awww, I'm sure you will," Mrs. Armstrong told her. "I don't want to keep you from doing what you're doing, so go ahead and get yourself situated."

"This turned out to be a lot easier than I thought it would be," Erica said, smiling. "I'm already beginning to feel at home."

"What did you think it would be like?" Mrs. Armstrong said while resting her hand on her hip.

"I don't know," said Erica. "I just didn't think it would be this comfortable...I didn't know if we'd have anything in common."

"Why, because we're Christians?"

"Sort of," Erica said honestly. "I guess you could say that. I just thought you were going to be uppity."

"You've been knowing us all your life, Erica. I know you haven't been around us all that much, but you should know enough to know we're not uppity."

"I know, but I guess I was too young to make an assessment," she said, feeling a bit uneasy.

"Baby, we're normal people just like everybody else—we just happen to be people who believes in God."

"I see," responded Erica. "I believe in him too, but I still have doubts about certain things—I guess my faith just isn't as strong as y'alls. At least not yet."

"It takes time, baby," Mrs. Armstrong told her. "You can't rush perfection. Give it some more time and you'll be okay, but don't forget you have to work on it constantly."

Erica looked at the woman who appeared to be flawless, wondering if she was being genuinely sincere, or was it all an act. "You are so easy to talk to," she said truthfully. "Talking to you is like talking to one of my girlfriends, or maybe even the sister I've never had."

"You and your mom didn't talk?"

"Not like this," she said with emphasis. "How could we when she was never around?"

"That's sad," Mrs. Armstrong told her. "I'm glad my husband and I are able to be here for you—I'd rather you be here with us than out in the streets."

"Me too," Erica said softly. "I guess God does work in mysterious ways."

"Yes, he does, and I'm so thankful for it," Mrs. Armstrong said as she looked up, seeing nothing but the ceiling staring back at her. "You seem to be a very nice young lady."

"Thank you. I try," said Erica.

"Smart, articulate and very polite. I guess you can say you're like the daughter I never had."

"See, I told you," Erica said, grinning.

"You did," said Mrs. Armstrong. "What happened between you and your mom that made her reach her breaking point? Why was she so adamant about putting you out?"

Erica paused before answering the question. She wasn't sure if Mrs. Armstrong could handle the truth. "Do I really have to tell you?" she asked shyly.

"No, not if you don't want to," replied Mrs. Armstrong. "But I wouldn't have asked if I didn't want to know."

"She came home unexpectedly one day and caught me having sex. It was a threesome, so I guess she couldn't handle the idea of me being with another girl."

"Oh, Lord," Mrs. Armstrong said. "I wasn't quite expecting to hear that, but I guess I kind of set myself up for it."

"It's not like I went out of my way to do it on purpose," the teen explained. "My mom's the kind of mother that's never home, so I wasn't expecting her to show up that day."

"The past is the past," said Mrs. Armstrong. "It wouldn't make sense to dwell on it now."

"You are so cool," Erica said, smiling. "I can already see we're going to be okay."

Mrs. Armstrong smiled. She had never played the role of mother before, so it made her feel good to be considered as *cool*. "I think we will, too. It's good to have you in my home, Miss Erica. I know we've already been down this road before, so, for the second time, I'm going to go ahead and let you get situated. There will be plenty of time for girl-talk later."

"I'll see you in a lil' while, Mrs. Armstrong," Erica said as her smile broadened. "Thanks again for welcoming me into your home. I can already tell it's going to be cool."

"Thank God not me," the older woman said as she walked toward the door. "It was he who put it on our hearts to take you in, so he's the one who deserves all the praise," she said before leaving the bedroom and pulling the door shut, her smile dissipated immediately when she entered the hallway.

Erica smiled to herself when she sat on the bed. She was really impressed with Mrs. Armstrong. *Thank you, Jesus* she said to herself as she got up to put the rest of her things away. She had never gotten so comfortable so quickly in a new environment, her new residence felt like the perfect sanctuary.

It wasn't long before she started having some serious doubts.

CHAPTER 3

Three weeks after seventeen-year-old Erica Miles moved into the Armstrong residence, the real Mrs. Armstrong started to emerge. The mean one, the spiteful—territorial one, the one who knit-picked and griped about everything—always wanting to know what everyone was doing.

Erica began to feel claustrophobic when she maneuvered throughout the house or around the church, because she knew Mrs. Armstrong was lurking around a corner, trying her best to shadow her every move. She felt the older woman's behavior was triggered by her breaking her curfew a couple of times during the first week, coming home reeking of marijuana and alcohol—a couple of bad habits she was still struggling to break.

The teen found it difficult to cut ties with her old acquaintances, but besides the few kinks and flaws that still needed to be ironed out, she felt everything else was going fine. She'd begun her new job as the church's accountant and, so far, her and Pastor Armstrong were getting along great.

She was grateful that Pastor Armstrong didn't condone his wife's nagging behavior, but she knew there wasn't much he could do about it. She witnessed him do everything in his power to keep her and his wife from being at each other's throat, but it became somewhat like a balancing act for him, because in order for him to appear fair, he couldn't afford to show favor toward one or the other. His wife was extremely upset by it and was constantly giving him the cold shoulder. She expressed to him on several occasions, that whether she be right or wrong, he was obligated to always side with her, but Pastor Armstrong disagreed.

He and Erica sat inside his office after services one Sunday afternoon while his wife was at the hospital visiting a sick friend. Things always seemed to go smoother when she was away, no tempers flaring, no attitudes—the entire environment seemed to be stress-free.

"You're doing a terrific job, young lady," the pastor said while putting the afternoon's earnings inside the safe. "Your numbers are always right, and you're doing it at a much faster pace than my wife was."

"I appreciate the compliment, but your way of doing things are so old-fashioned," the teen replied.

"What's old-fashioned about it?" inquired the pastor.

"No one uses ledgers or logbooks to do anything anymore. You can keep track of every dollar earned and spent if you invest in a computer. There's software that's perfect for this kind of stuff."

"I don't do computers; I'm too old for that," he said, annoyed.

"You're not old, Pastor Armstrong. You're just a man who's stuck in his ways," the teen told him.

"You're right about that," he said, smiling. "The log works for me, so I see no need in changing it."

"If you say so," Erica said under her breath.

Pastor Armstrong stared at the teen. There was something about her that he found intriguing. "You're pretty good at keeping the books, young lady, I'm sure my wife would be impressed by it."

"Thank you," Erica said stoically, immediately recognizing the opportunity to voice her opinion. "Nothing about me would impress your wife, it'll probably only make her hate me more."

"She doesn't hate you," Pastor Armstrong responded.

"Shh, I can't tell," Erica interjected. "If she liked me, she wouldn't be putting me through what she puts me through."

"Just like you said about me, she's just a woman who's set in her ways," the pastor said before continuing. "I don't think she's too comfortable having a younger woman around. I can't explain why, but I think she sees you as a potential threat."

"Why would I be a threat?" the teen said defensively.

"You being younger and prettier is the only thing I can think of," Pastor Armstrong said. "That's how she felt about Danielle at first."

"Danielle is beautiful," Erica said. "You do know she's gay, right?"

"Of course I do. That's the only thing that puts my wife at ease."

"Why the hell did she invite me to come stay with y'all then?"

"Well, that was mostly my idea," the pastor admitted. "It was me who didn't want to see you end up in a shelter or out on the streets, so I did what I felt like I had to do."

"Oh," Erica said with her head down, wondering why he'd gone out on a limb for her. "If I was her, I would probably see me as a threat too. I think she knows she's not handling her business."

Pastor Armstrong was caught off guard. He didn't understand what the teen was implying, so he urged her to elaborate. "Besides being my wife, what else do you assume she's supposed to be doing?"

"Well, it's just my personal opinion, but I don't think she's doing a good job of being your wife!" she said audaciously, hoping she hadn't over-stepped her boundaries.

"I beg your pardon?" winced the pastor.

Erica knew she'd come too far to back down, the only thing she could do was press forward. "She's not doing what a real wife is supposed to be doing."

Again, Pastor Armstrong was stumped; he had no idea what was being insinuated. "What on God's earth are you talking about? Please share with me what you think you know."

Erica knew she had said too much, but she still refused to back down. "Well, pastor, you have to remember my bedroom is not too far from yours. The walls are paper-thin, and not once have I heard you guys being intimate with each other," she stated boldly. "My question to you is this, does she know the importance of pleasing her man?"

"Young lady, you're way out of line. I don't think it's none of your business! What happens between my wife and me is between us. You have no idea what we do in private, but whatever we do, is none of your business."

"You're right. I'm sorry," Erica said quickly. "It wasn't my intention to butt into you guys' business, but since you and I were having a discussion, I thought it was cool to express my observation. I guess I was wrong. I'm sorry."

"And what observation is that?" inquired the pastor.

"I only asked if she knew the importance of pleasing her man because I sense you're not having your needs met. Maybe I'm wrong?" she said in a low voice.

Pastor Armstrong was taken aback by the young woman's boldness. He struggled to formulate the words to express his discomfort. "Young lady, I think you should learn how to stay in your place. This is adult stuff, when you become an adult, you'll understand."

The pastor of Real Love Baptist Church was extremely uncomfortable discussing a topic so personal with his young new-hire, but the teen was correct about her assumption.

It had been quite some time since he and his wife had been intimate. Every time he attempted to show her any affection she would always give him the cold shoulder—it was something they argued about constantly. "I think this conversation is over. Now if you don't mind, I need to prepare for tonight's service."

"Okay," Erica said as she got up to leave. She was confident that the seed she wanted to plant had been planted; all she had to do now was sit back and let it germinate.

Pastor Armstrong watched the over-developed teen as she left his office. He had never met a young person so wise and mature, it made him begin to second-guess his decision.

Erica stormed from his office and entered the empty church. She was just about to call a friend to come pick her up when her cell phone began vibrating inside her hand. "Hello."

"What's up, ma. What's wrong?"

"Nothin'."

"You sure? I see you down there lookin' sad."

"Nah, I'm not sad," responded Erica. "Just got a few things on my mind right now."

"Come up here to chill so we can talk about it."

Erica looked toward the balcony hesitantly. Then she said, "Alright."

Moments later she was up on the balcony with her co-worker Danielle, who was stretched out on a bench with her ankles crossed. They hung out together quite often while at the church, but they rarely discussed anything about their personal lives. They discussed fashion and the latest gossip, mainly consisting of who was messing around with whom inside the congregation.

"I haven't seen you look this uncomfortable since the day you walked in here," Danielle said while staring at Erica. "What happened in there?"

"Nothin'."

"C'mon, ma. Did he try coming on to you in there?"

"Hell no!" Erica said, offended. "Why would you ask me something like that?"

"I'm just sayin'. I'm trying to find out what's bothering you."

"It ain't no shit like that," the teen said with emphasis. "I'm just tired of Mrs. Armstrong fuckin' with me. I tried to get him to make her calm down."

"What's she doin'?"

"Talkin' shit, basically. The bitch be following me everywhere I go, wondering what I'm doing, who I'm hanging out with—all that stupid ass shit."

"Dang, ma. You're on one," Danielle said, sympathetically. "I knew something had to be bothering you, but I didn't think it would be Sister Willa."

"That old bitch be trippin'," Erica said with a giggle. "I can't figure out what to do about her, and the pastor acts like he's scared of her," she said laughing.

"That's what I'm talkin' about, ma. Let me see that smile," Danielle said, hoping to change the subject. "Ma, you look so much better when you smile. I don't like seeing you lookin' all down and shit. Don't let temporary shit get the best of you."

"Oh, you do cuss?" Erica said, surprised.

"Of course I do, don't we all?"

"I've never heard you do it so I wasn't sure."

"Oh, don't get it twisted. I'm from the streets. I just work at the church. I do a lot of things you don't know about. We might have a lot more in common than you think, ma."

"What's up with this *ma* shit? Where you from?"

"Brooklyn," she said proudly.

"I figured it had to be New York or New Jersey, 'cause we don't talk like that out here. That shit sounds kind of cool though, we need to step our game up on this West Coast."

"You think?" Danielle said, smiling.

"It's alright," said Erica, not wanting to make her think too high of herself. She wanted to tell Danielle how pretty she was, but decided against it, because she didn't want the woman to get the wrong impression.

"You like my get-down?" she said again. "I appreciate it, ma. I take that as a compliment."

"It is," Erica said, smiling.

"Thank you again," Danielle told her.

"I know I'm switchin' subjects, but do you and Ne-Ne talk much?"

Ne-Ne was once a troubled teen the pastor met while doing charity work at a homeless shelter six years prior. He didn't move her into his residence like he did Erica, but she was known as the fix-it girl when she was at the homeless shelter, so he hired her to do maintenance around the church.

"I talk to her sometimes. Why?"

"I'm just askin'," said Erica. "That bitch is so strange to me. Walking around here with all of those damn keys and tools on her tool belt, looking like some kind of mechanic or something."

Danielle knew exactly what Erica was talking about, so she burst into laughter before replying. "That bitch do be lookin' like she'll lay on her back and slide up under a car."

Both girls continued laughing. They agreed that Ne-Ne was a strange character. With so many keys dangling from her tool belt, they heard her coming from a mile away.

"I'm sorry but I gotta cut this short, Danielle. I gotta go ahead and get my ass out of here. Gotta get ready to go deal with this evil bitch. I'll leave you here to deal with this weirdo."

"You got a ride?"

"Nope," said Erica.

"Girl, this is the west side, you don't need to be by yourself walking down these streets. Hold on a minute, I'll take you home."

"I'm born and raised on these streets, I don't fear none of this nice ass shit," the teen said.

"You're somethin' else," Danielle said with a smile.

Erica looked back over her shoulder before saying, "I know."

CHAPTER 4

It became clear to the pastor of Real Love Baptist Church that his wife and Erica could no longer reside under the same roof. Meaningless catfights ensued on a daily basis—nearly all of them provoked by Mrs. Armstrong. It was always one thing or another. Whether it be this or that, she seemed to always find something to complain about.

Pastor Armstrong gave Erica a lot of credit. He thought she did a terrific job of exercising restraint and poise each time she was wrongly approached by his aggressive wife, who seemed to get meaner and grumpier with each day that passed. He felt Erica displayed an exceptional amount of control and obedience, considering her youth and inexperience, but to Mrs. Armstrong, she viewed everything the teen did as immature and unacceptable.

It didn't matter to the older woman that their young houseguest did more than her share when it came to chores. Erica cleaned the kitchen, her bedroom and bathroom, washed loads of laundry that wasn't her own, even tidied up the garage a couple of times, not once did she ever complain, but Mrs. Armstrong appreciated none of it. The only thing she cleaned was she and her husband's bedroom and bathroom—the house had two master bedrooms, so if a guest had to use the restroom, they used the one inside of

Erica's room. Nothing Erica did was satisfactory to her—Mrs. Armstrong just preferred to have her gone.

The woman and teenager were in the midst of a heated argument when Erica reached her breaking point and stormed out of the front door. Pastor Armstrong stayed inside to console his angry wife before heading outside to discuss matters with Erica. It wasn't the first time he had seen the teen avoid a physical altercation with his hostile wife, so he knew she wouldn't go much farther than the front yard.

He spotted her sitting in a lawn chair beside the garden, so he strode across the lawn and sat next to her. "How's it going, young lady?" he asked calmly.

The mature teenager didn't respond. She didn't feel a response was necessary since she was more than certain he knew the answer, she wasn't in the mood for any small talk.

"You do know it's going to be okay, don't you?" he said in a soothing tone.

"I'm tired of going through this," Erica said, on the verge of tears. "I could have stayed at my mom's if I wanted to go through this."

"I hate it too, young lady, believe me."

Erica was surprised by the pastor's answer. She knew he was stuck between a rock and a hard place, but she was more than elated to see he'd sided with her. "I guess there is a god," she said with a smile before wiping her eyes.

"Of course there is, and he wants you to know that everything will be fine."

"I hope so," Erica said as she leaned forward with her head down, unknowingly exposing her ample cleavage.

"Oh, I know so," Pastor Armstrong told her. "You need to start having more faith, young lady. Start giving God the credit he deserves, start spending more time talking to him in prayer."

Erica didn't respond. She wasn't sure how she was supposed to, so she let Pastor Armstrong continue talking.

"Most times God can easily step in and fix everything for us, but he be waiting for us to hand it all over to him, but it never crosses our minds to do it," he said. "We try to handle everything ourselves when we really need to call and depend on him. He's the only one we can truly count on."

"I'm sure you're right, but right now I'm stressed out. Dealing with this drama every day is becoming too much for me. Way too much," the teen said, ignoring the pastor.

"You're too blessed to be stressed and too anointed to be disappointed," said Pastor Armstrong. "God wants you to know that everything is fine. He knows what your problems are and has already worked everything out for you."

"Something has to change; I can't keep putting up with her messing with me."

"She won't be bothering you anymore," the pastor told her.

Erica contemplated that statement. The teen liked Pastor Armstrong a lot, specifically his confidence and positive attitude, but she felt his words were only rhetoric in a desperate attempt to make her feel good. "Are you telling me you're going to make a miracle happen?"

"I'm not at liberty to step on God's toes. He's in the miracle-working business, not me. That's handled already," he said while staring at her. "When's the last time you called on him?"

"Today. I asked him to keep your wife out my face," she said, giggling. "She's on my back about everything. You see how she acts; I'd probably choke her out if you weren't around."

Pastor Armstrong smiled. The teen didn't pull any punches. She wasn't afraid to say exactly what she meant, that's one of the things that he liked about her. "Well, you can start thanking God for answering your prayer."

"Answered it how, my situation is still the same?"

"Not for long," he said before elaborating. "I'm tired of seeing you and my wife go at it, so I'm going to get you your own apartment."

She was certain he was toying with her, and she didn't like it. "Stop playing." Getting her own apartment was the farthest thing from her mind. It sounded too good to be true.

"I'm not playing," he assured her. "My wife says she wants you out. She doesn't care where you go, but just so you won't think we're in collusion, I'm not going to throw you out on the streets or anything like that, instead, I'm going to put you in your own place."

UNGODLY

Erica leaned forward and gave the pastor a long hug. In the one month that she lived with the Christian couple, she really developed a profound respect for him. He turned out to be a man of his word. She was of the opinion, that any man who kept his word was a man of great character—he really meant it when he told Lisa he would take good care of her.

Erica was undoubtedly grateful to him for taking her in and felt even more indebted to him because he'd taken an interest in her that her own father hadn't dared to. She found herself at a loss for words. She had never even dreamed of having her own apartment, now here she was, about to get one. "Thank you, Pastor Armstrong," she said in a joyous voice. "I don't know how I'm ever going to repay you for this, but I'm sure I'll be trying to come up with something."

"Thank God not me," he said calmly, not knowing his wife had uttered the exact words a month prior. "We'll go look for you a place first thing in the morning. Try to get along with her for one more night."

"Thank you," she said before hugging him again. The teen was more excited than she'd ever been. She wouldn't turn eighteen for another four months, and already, she was getting her own apartment. She couldn't have been happier.

CHAPTER 5

Tuesday morning was beautiful for young Erica Miles. It was the kind of day that jogged the memory of the last day of school, when most teenagers looked forward to three months of fun.

The beautiful scented moisture of freshly cut grass blended perfectly with the fragrances of red and yellow roses and sweet cherry blossoms—producing a soothing atmosphere that only summer could bring.

It was the kind of day that drew out the prettiest creatures. Plump golden colored honeybees swarmed harmoniously through the winds with bright red ladybugs and immaculately painted butterflies, gliding from flower to flower, being rewarded with more than their share of pollen and nectar. Hummingbirds flapped their wings gallantly but silently while hovering over plants like Black Hawk helicopters, using their long narrow beaks to sift its nectar.

Erica smiled after loading her belongings into the trunk of the pastor's car. She felt more vibrant than she had in a long time as she strolled from the rear to the passenger side door before climbing inside, carrying only her purse.

She was glad to be out of Mrs. Armstrong's hair, and was quite sure the older woman was just as relieved. *Thank god that's over* she said to herself as Pastor Armstrong turned the ignition and pulled away from the curb.

She looked at the house from the corner of her eyes and was more than certain that Mrs. Armstrong was peeking through one of the blinds. The woman was always lurking around a corner like the Grim Reaper, as if she trusted nothing or no one, other than herself.

Erica pulled a paperback from her purse, snatched the bookmark from between its pages, reclined in her seat and began reading.

"That sure doesn't look like the Bible, young lady," Pastor Armstrong said as he reached over to look at the book's cover. "Terrence Brothers— Unduly Sworn. I don't think I've ever heard of him."

"He's one of my favorite authors," the teen replied while using her long fingernail to mark the spot where she stopped reading. "This dude is relatable. Everything he writes about are things that happen for real."

"I can tell by the cover that it wouldn't be something I'd wanna read," the pastor said.

"You shouldn't knock something you haven't tried," replied Erica. "That's exactly why they say you should never judge a book by its cover. The genre he writes is more like reality-fiction, it's entertaining and truthful at the same time," she said while thumbing through the pages.

"Things like what?" he said dryly.

"Things like life," she said with emphasis. "His novels Unethical 1 & 2 addresses HIV/AIDS, Unfair 1 & 2 talks about the racial injustices that exists in the American judicial system, and this one is about racism and corruption on the highest levels. I've read all of his stuff—I'm telling you they're some good books."

"Racial injustice and corruption?" Pastor Armstrong uttered, distastefully. "What race is he?"

"Black," she said as she flipped the book over so he could see the author's photo on the back cover. "He wrote all of these books while sitting in prison."

"That's good," the pastor said. "At least he's using his time wisely. It's not the Bible, but I'm glad to see you're reading something. We've come a long way as a people in this country, but not far enough. You're a young black girl who enjoys reading and is actually reading a book by a black author. That was almost unheard of when I was growing up."

"Reading relaxes me," the teen stated. "It helps me escape reality when I need to, but I have a lot of friends who don't like to read. I don't get that."

"I don't understand it either," the pastor said as he turned a corner. "There was a time in American history when black folks were hung for trying to learn how to read or write. Now that it's available to us in all sorts of ways, a lot of us still choose not to take advantage of it."

"Well, I love it," Erica said, proudly. "I honestly can't imagine my life without it. Reading to me opens up a whole new world."

"That's good…glad to hear that," the pastor told her. "You're an exceptional young woman; I'm proud of you."

"Thank you," she said as she glanced at him.

"Let me ask you this though…how many blacks do you know that don't know how to read or write?"

She thought about some of her old classmates and began naming them off one by one. "This girl named Shannon…Tamika…Shaun…Tanya…Demetrius…I know quite a few."

"Okay, now name someone white you know who can't read."

Erica became quiet as she thought about it. She thought long and hard trying to come up with a name, but her mind couldn't seem to produce one. "I can't think of anybody," she finally said.

"My point exactly," the pastor stated. "I've been on this earth sixty-two years, and as unbelievable as it may sound, I've never met a white person who couldn't read."

"That's crazy," said Erica.

"White folks know the importance of it, so they don't let their people go through life like that. Blacks, yes, whites, no," the pastor said as he glanced at Erica, noticing her nipple protruding through her form-fitting shirt. "They used to say 'if you wanna hide something from a black, all you gotta do is put it in a book.'"

"Uh," she said when she caught his gaze, but played it off coolly like she didn't notice.

"That's because they knew a lot of us couldn't read, but now that we can, a lot of us still won't crack open a book."

"Sad but true," the teen agreed. "I've heard that expression before, but you said something earlier that I'm struggling to understand."

"What's that?" the pastor said anxiously.

"You said it's not the Bible I'm reading, so my question is this, if white people were killing blacks for trying to learn how to read or write, why did they allow us to learn the Bible if it was really something that was going to benefit us as a people?" she said before pausing. "I mean, it's hard for me to believe that the same people who were intentionally holding us back would have given us something that was going to help us move forward. Doesn't that seem contradictory to you?"

The elderly pastor had no response. He'd heard the analogy before, but it was simply a question that he couldn't answer—he side stepped it quickly and pushed past it. "God works in mysterious ways, young lady. He has a purpose for everything that happens, a lot of it is beyond our comprehension."

"But doesn't it seem like the Bible was just a tool they used to control black people mentally? They say if you can control the mind you can control the body. We see proof every day that white people are in control of our minds, so, in reality, they control our bodies—we put ourselves exactly where they want us."

"And what proof are you relying on?" the pastor said, frowning.

"Well, for one, white people told us that our rightful place was in the back of the bus, right? Now to this day if we get on a bus, most of us will automatically go to the back of it. When I was in school, I actually saw people fight each other over the back seat—who in their right mind would do that?"

"Yeah, I've seen it too," the pastor admitted. "It was a long time ago, but I've definitely seen it. What's another one?"

"Um, white people told us we're niggers, right? Now it's turned into an epidemic. Not only are we happily calling ourselves and each other that—both in public and private—but it's loosely used in our favorite movies and music and broadcast to the world like it's okay to say."

"Yeah, I don't want to talk about racism though," he said with a sigh. "I'm past that, and I think all blacks need to get over it. We haven't figured out how to get ahead in life 'cause we're too busy holding ourselves back, blaming other people for our shortcomings."

Erica immediately looked toward the pastor, holding her hand up while shaking her head. "I have to strongly disagree with you on that one. Us calling ourselves the 'N' word is not helping us at all. Don't get me wrong, I agree it's a terrible word and we shouldn't be using it, but it's not the blame for our setbacks," she said. "We're not the ones in charge of financial institutions; banks, credit unions, the institutions of higher learning, the corporations and franchises, the real estate and stock markets. We don't run any of these entities, so you can't say that we're holding ourselves back. Those are the entities we need to get ahead in life, but we can't get ahead if they don't let us in…"

Pastor Armstrong couldn't refute what the teen had said. He didn't understand how she was so knowledgeable. "You've gone out of my league on that, young lady. I wouldn't have a clue how to answer any of that. I don't even know what some of that stuff means."

"What about Christians?" she continued.

"What about us?"

"White people told us we're Christians and Baptists. A lot of us call ourselves one or the other, but I don't think we really know what either of them mean," she said rapidly. "We really can't explain the differences between the two, or its origin, but we say we're one or the other because our mom or dad told us that's what we are."

"Right."

"They got it from their parents, their parents got it from white people—now, besides those who are Muslim or Rastafarian, the majority of blacks call themselves Christian or Baptist. That's crazy."

"Young lady, you really have some serious questions and, unfortunately, I won't be able to answer them for you," he said as he turned into a parking lot, parking in front of an office building. "You need to pray and ask God to give you understanding. Right now, it's time to see your new place."

Erica got out of the car and looked around. She didn't like how old and decrepit the buildings looked—the neighborhood appeared to be far from peaceful. "Wow," she said as she forced a smile. "This isn't really what I was expecting, but I'm not in a position to be picky, am I?"

"Oh, you'll be okay," Pastor Armstrong told her as he removed her belongings from the trunk of his car. "An old buddy of mine manages this property, plus it's the only thing I can afford to get you right now."

"What about furniture and stuff?" she said, sounding a bit ungrateful.

"It's already furnished," the pastor told her. "You'll just have to make due until something better comes along. I just made the call to him yesterday, so this was sort of put together on short notice."

"I'm not complaining. I would hate to sound unappreciative. I mean, it's not the ideal apartment I had in mind, but it has to be better than being at your place. At least I won't have to deal with crazy lady."

"On that note, this place should bring you plenty of peace."

"Thank god for that. I need that more than anything," she said happily.

The two entered the front office carrying Erica's belongings, appearing as though they were at a cheap motel.

"Good morning, pastor. This must be the lovely young lady you told me about?" the apartment manager said as he immediately approached.

"It is," Pastor Armstrong said as they shook hands. "Larry, this is Erica. Erica, this is Larry."

"Hi, Erica," he said as he reached for her hand. "The pastor told me a few things about you, but he failed to mention you were this good looking."

"Thank you," Erica said blushing, noticing how disgustingly tight the man's pants were.

"Don't even think about it, Larry. Just focus on what I asked you to do for me. I already told you she's underage," Pastor Armstrong said in Erica's defense.

"No problem," he said with a stoic expression after noticing the anger in the pastor's voice. Larry Kokane was a slim brown-complexioned man in his mid-fifties, who truly believed he had a way with words. He and the pastor were not strangers. He was actually an ex-boyfriend of Willa Armstrong's before her and Pastor Armstrong met at a club. The two men were once arch enemies before setting their differences aside, realizing that no woman was worth fighting over, especially a woman like Willa Armstrong, who once had an unquenchable appetite for drugs and sex.

"Is everything set up?" the pastor asked.

"Everything's done," the apartment manager said. "Since she's a minor, all you gotta do is sign these papers as her co-signer. She has to put her signature below yours, then you two can get the key and be on your way."

"Sounds good," Pastor Armstrong said as he and Erica followed the manager to the front counter.

"I already got the papers ready for you. Sign next to the X's—here, here, here, and here," he said, using his index finger as a pointer before handing him a pen. "Everything inside the unit is clean as a whistle. My janitor Nino said everything is in perfect working condition so if you have a problem with anything just let me know."

The pastor and Erica just nodded their heads as they signed the lease and slid it back to him.

"You're in apartment 7, Miss Erica Miles. It's a downstairs unit just up the sidewalk," Larry said while skimming over their signatures—pointing toward the sidewalk in front of the office.

"Wait for me outside, young lady. I'll be out there in a few minutes," Pastor Armstrong told her. He waited for Erica to sit all of her belongings outside the front office before turning back toward the apartment manager. "Larry, no one who asks is to know where this young lady is staying."

"Is there anyone in particular I should be aware of?"

"No, not really," the pastor told him. "But, just in case, I want you to know that her whereabouts is to stay between us."

"No problem," said Larry KoKane. "None of this is any of my business. I'm just providing her with a safe place to stay like you asked me to. I've done my part so I'm out of it," he said as he dangled the key in front of him.

"My man," Pastor Armstrong said. "It's cool for her mom to know though. You do remember Lisa Miles, don't you?"

"Oh, that's whose daughter that is?" Larry said with regret. He had recently seen Lisa at a nearby convenience store where she offered him sex for money. He assumed she was looking to score some drugs, he wanted nothing at all to do with her.

"Yeah, that's her daughter, but don't forget, she's off limits," he said as a warning. "The first and last month's rent is inside this envelope, plus a hundred-dollar tip for making this happen on such a short notice."

"You got it, fam. Anytime," the man said as they shook hands.

Pastor Armstrong pushed outside where Erica was waiting for him. He picked up two of her three bags and let her grab the remaining one before making their way toward apartment 7.

Erica was impressed when they went inside. She was reminded of the advice she had just given to the pastor to never judge a book by its cover. The apartment was not only huge but was also immaculate—more modern looking internally than it was externally—everything was much better than she thought it would be. The furniture was beautiful and well placed. From her and the pastor's disposition, all they saw was beautiful hardwood floors—a welcomed sight to Erica, because she hated the ugly brown or beige carpet that usually covered apartment floors, like the tacky pecan-colored carpet that was spread throughout her mother's apartment.

The floor, walls and furniture were all clean. Everything seemed to emanate that *brand-new* smell.

"I love this," Erica said as she walked around, inspecting behind every cabinet and door that she came across. "Thank you, Pastor Armstrong. I can't believe I got my own apartment."

"I'm glad you like it," he said, appeased. "I'm glad I was able to do this for you."

"It's so peaceful—listen," she said before smiling. "Thank you."

"You're welcome," he said as they embraced. "We'll work on getting you a driver's license and getting you a car next. For now, I'll pick you up for work every day, plus drop you back off—everything else will work itself out."

The thought of getting her own car was too much for her to bear; both of her eyes quickly filled with tears, she stretched out her arms to hug him again. "Thank you so much for caring. You have no idea how much this means to me."

"I know it means a lot to you, sweetheart, but it couldn't have happened without God."

"Thank you, Jesus—Thank you, God," she said aloud.

She smiled as she wiped away her tears, looking around again at her new apartment. "I need to start putting my things away and get used to the idea of having my own spot."

"Go ahead and get everything squared away," Pastor Armstrong told her. "I'll come back later so we can go get your necessities...food...pots and pans...dishes...cleaning supplies and whatever else you may need to get yourself situated."

"I'll be waiting," Erica said with her hand on her well-developed hip, not having an inkling of how sexy he thought she looked.

Pastor Armstrong gave her one last hug before leaving her alone, but not before making it clear that she wasn't to have any visitors. "Teamwork makes a dream work, so let's focus on getting your life on track."

"You're awesome, Pastor Armstrong," she said, smiling. "You really have a way with words. I can see now why that lady is so crazy about you."

"I'll see you in a lil' bit," he said, ignoring her comment.

"See you then."

Erica locked the front door once the pastor left, then looked around once more and burst out laughing. She couldn't believe the direction her life was headed, and she couldn't have been prouder of herself.

CHAPTER 6

Danielle was hesitant when she pulled the door open to let her visitor inside before returning to the kitchen of her two-bedroom home. Her red laced teddy-like nightgown rested perfectly between her well-proportioned backside and the small of her back as she stood in front of the sink to finish washing the dishes. It really hadn't been a good day for her, so she really didn't feel like being bothered with company.

A few days prior, she returned home after working at the church and found a hand-written note smack dead in the center of her front door from the president of her neighborhood's Home Owners Association, giving her seventy-two hours to get her yard in compliance. Her job at the church prevented her from doing it sooner—she had to wait until her day off.

She was already struggling financially—underwater in bills, so she couldn't afford to hire someone to do it like she had in the past—something she deeply regretted, because the HOA had really become a nuisance to her. She spent most of the day in the scorching sun pulling weeds, mowing the lawn, trimming the hedges, and scraping up a huge oil stain from the center of her driveway to avoid being hit with a hefty fine.

UNGODLY

After taking a long hot shower, she ate leftover pepperoni and cheese pizza from the night before then chased it down with a half bottle of red wine. She had plans of going to bed as soon as she finished the dishes, but a disturbing phone call had taken her off course.

"Tell me what I wanna know, Danielle," her visitor said from behind her.

"C'mon, ma. I don't know why you still chose to come over here when I told you on the phone that I don't know nothin'.'"

"Because I know you're lying to me."

"No I'm not," Danielle said without turning around.

"Danielle, I've been your age before, you've never been mine," the visitor replied. "I know when someone is lying or telling the truth."

Danielle heard her visitor's footsteps getting closer behind her, but instead of turning around to face her unwelcomed guest, she proceeded to wash and rinse the remaining dishes that were inside the sink before placing them inside a dish rack that was already overloaded, in a desperate attempt to avoid a confrontation. "If that were true you wouldn't have came over here."

"I know that little girl told you something, Danielle," the visitor said, refusing to take no for an answer.

"I'm tellin' you, ma, she didn't," Danielle repeated. She pulled the cork from the sink to drain the water, then felt her visitor's body press firmly against her buttocks, followed by warm soft lips against her neck. "You know I would tell you if I knew something, ma."

The woman saw no need to continue speaking. She sucked Danielle's earlobe inside her warm wet mouth, then ran the tip of her tongue in circles inside her ear.

Danielle's knees nearly buckled to the woman's touch; she became receptive as she leaned into her; her own vagina began to moisten. "Oooh, that feels good, ma. I miss that."

"I miss it too," the woman said as she slipped her hand inside Danielle's panties from the back and began stimulating her overly engorged clitoris with the tip of her middle finger, then slipped it inside her.

It had been a while since Danielle had received that kind of affection. She leaned forward over the kitchen sink, allowing her female visitor to finger her deeply. "Oooh, that feels so good, ma. Damn!" she said between breaths. Danielle turned around in search of the woman's lips, when she found them, she began kissing her slowly and deeply, then seductively sucked her own juices off the woman's fingers. Before long, they were sprawled out naked across the kitchen floor, kissing and licking all over each other, until they simultaneously reached a powerful orgasm.

"Damn, Danielle, that pussy still taste good. I almost forgot how good that tongue feels."

"You taste good too, ma," Danielle said, panting. "It's been a long time since I came that hard."

"Me too, you still got my pussy throbbing. Here feel it," the woman said as she spread her legs placing Danielle's fingers inside her vagina. "I hadn't had an orgasm in a long time before tonight. It's been a while since my husband got some of this, we argue about it nearly every day."

"Do you think it's fair, he's your husband?"

"I know it's not."

"But, if he went out and got sex elsewhere, you'd think he's wrong?"

"We're not going there. I might go home and give him some tonight."

"Well, I'm serious about Erica not telling me nothin'," Danielle said. "She hasn't told me about anything he's done that was out of line. I think he genuinely cares for her."

"It has to be more to it than that, her little fast ass just hasn't told you yet."

"I pray there's nothin' to tell me," Danielle said before she climbed from the floor, helping her guest to her feet. They embraced each other once more before getting dressed. It had been a year since they'd been intimate with each other, and for reasons unknown, they were already regretting their latest encounter.

Danielle knew since childhood about her sexuality, but her visitor stumbled upon it accidentally a year and a half earlier when Danielle seduced her on the church's balcony. Danielle was the only woman she'd ever been with, but she was extremely uncomfortable engaging in such ungodly behavior, especially since she'd turned her life around.

"Goodnight, Danielle," the woman said without making eye contact. "Let me know if you find out something."

"Goodnight to you too, Sister Willa. You'll be the first to know if I hear something."

"Thank you. Enjoy the rest of your night."

"You too, ma. I'll see you tomorrow," Danielle said before she closed the door. Immediately after she turned the lock, Danielle went to her bedroom and drank the rest of her wine, then reached into the drawer of her nightstand next to her bed, pulled out her battery-operated friend and brought herself to another climax before going to bed.

CHAPTER 7

Emotions ran way above normal at Real Love Baptist Church when Pastor Buddy Armstrong finished delivering another one of his powerful sermons. He preached a message about forgiveness, and how important it is for human beings to forgive each other. Everyone was on the brink of sadness when the pastor took a seat, but it was a thirty-six-year-old guest speaker by the name of Sydney, who'd recently been released from prison, who pushed emotions over the top when he gave his heartbreaking testimony about his own mother betraying him by having him arrested and sent to prison when he was eighteen-years-old. He explained how she secretly called the police on him early one morning after a total stranger told her he'd committed a robbery. When the cops arrived at his mom's home, she watched as they heartlessly and callously cuffed his wrists tightly behind his back, slammed him down on the living room floor and began beating and stomping him for no reason at all.

The young man described how the two white police officers unrelentingly kicked, punched, and choked him in the presence of his mother, while she stood by watching without saying a word, as if the young man they were beating meant nothing to her.

He explained to the audience that he and his mom were awfully close before the incident, and that he'd been blindsided by her sudden betrayal. He described it by saying it felt like his heart had been ripped from his chest, making it nearly impossible for him to trust anyone for years, and how his love for her had temporarily turned into hate. He still hadn't learned how to fully forgive her. To make matters worse, she made him wait eighteen long antagonizing years after the incident before she finally came to her senses and apologized, but by that time it was too little too late, the irreparable damage was already done.

The young black man admitted during his testimony that his relationship with his mom would probably never be the same, and that it was only by the grace of God that they still had any kind of relationship.

Tears rolled down his face as he left the pulpit, the entire congregation openly wept with him. The choir ended the service with a series of heart-warming songs, while several members of the church held him up in prayer.

The ex-convict appeared to be well mannered and very polite—no one seemed to understand his mom's reasoning for doing what she did, but of course, it was probably because no one knew her side of the story?

Once services were over, Pastor Buddy Armstrong and his young accountant were inside his office, winding down and counting the day's offering, but for some odd reason, something felt different. Usually when they were alone inside his spacious office, they would use the time to engage in conversation that was mentally stimulating, something they couldn't seem to do when Mrs. Armstrong was around, but this time, they both seemed to be bothered and, after a long moment of silence, one of them finally spoke.

"Sydney's story was really touching, wasn't it?" said Pastor Armstrong, his voice going in and out like he needed some water. "If my mom had done something like that to me, I don't know if I'd ever be able to forgive her."

"I know I couldn't," Erica said while jotting down some numbers. "I wouldn't have a mom anymore, our mother/daughter relationship would be a wrap."

Pastor Armstrong knew the teen was serious. Even for a godly man, he believed a mother should never do anything to harm her child—he honestly understood the teen's position, but he decided to approach it from a different angle. "Time heals all wounds," he said, trying to sound obedient. "I know there's nothing our God can't do, sometimes we just have to let go and let God. We have to decrease ourselves to increase him. We just have to ask him to humble us."

Yeah, right Erica said to herself.

"We just have to learn how to trust and believe," he continued. "God will take care of everything if we allow him to."

"I don't buy into rhetoric or clichés like that," Erica said honestly. "Sometimes we just have to see and accept reality for what it is. Things are what they are, and we can't change that."

"Faith is to believe in things unseen," the pastor told her. "No matter how grim or bleak a situation might look, we just have to believe that our God will fix it."

"So, you're telling me that the unseen things carry more weight than the things we can see?" Erica said, looking at him out the corner of her eye.

"I'm just trying to stress the fact that we should have more faith," said Pastor Armstrong. "The Bible tells us to have faith, I'm just telling you what the book says."

"The Bible says a lot of things I don't necessarily agree with," Erica chanted. "It also says that all men were created equal, but we know it's not true."

"Says who? All men are created equal," the pastor retorted. "Why would you doubt that?"

"Because we see proof of it every day that contradicts it," replied Erica. "How in the hell are we created equal when some people are born blind while others can see? Some are born paraplegic while others have all of their limbs. Some are born with terminal illnesses like AIDS and cancer while others are born perfectly healthy. Some are born with high IQ's while others have learning disabilities. Should I go on?"

"No, I got the point," the pastor admitted. "I guess it's a valid argument, but God makes us equal in other ways. He has a perfect reason for doing everything he does. We might not always understand what his reasoning is, but anything that has to do with God may not be meant for us to understand."

Erica smiled as she shook her head. She knew Pastor Armstrong was in denial—every Christian she'd ever encountered was the same way. "I think God was presented to us wrong when we were kids," she began. "He was presented to us like he was some kind of genie in a bottle—I don't think he operates like that."

"God's love for us is unconditional. He promised to give us anything and everything we ask him for, but that's only if he thinks we're ready to receive it," the pastor said with his arms crossed.

"Well, I try not to ask him for anything, I just thank him for what he does for me."

"There's no harm in that, at least you know where your blessings come from."

"I do," said Erica. "You said a minute ago that God loves us unconditionally—why are there so many conditions in the Bible if that's the case?"

"They're not conditions," the pastor told her. "They're laws or instructions that the Lord wants us to live by."

"The Bible has our people so stupid," the teen retorted. "Those white people sure knew what the hell they were doing when they told our ancestors that it was a white man out there named Jesus Christ who would save us if we ask him to. Our people were oppressed and had nothing else to depend on in those days, so they clung to whatever those white folks threw at them. That's probably the reason why no other race believes in Jesus the way black people do. It's like we were in the middle of a lake drowning, and they knew we would grab hold of anything they threw at us, especially if we thought it was going to save us."

"You're wrong for doubting the power of our living God," the pastor said in frustration. "Do you not believe Jesus Christ died for your sins?"

"Do you really want to know my answer to that?"

"Oh, Lord," he said with his head down, knowing he wouldn't like her answer. "Go ahead and give me your take on it."

"Now you know people die every day, right?" she said while looking at him. "I know you do because you do funerals at this church almost every other weekend. My question is this; if Jesus died for us, why in the hell do we still have to die? If I bought you a plane ticket, that means you wouldn't have to pay for one yourself, all you'd have to do is get on the plane. Why in the hell do I still have to die if somebody else already died for me?"

Pastor Armstrong dreaded being asked questions of this nature. He knew most people lacked the audacity to ask such questions, but, again, he knew the teen had made a valid point. He sat on the corner of his desk staring down at the floor while his young audacious accountant stood inches away from him, her hand resting comfortably on her protruding hip.

"Pastor Armstrong, why do they say God doesn't put more on a person than that person can handle when we see all of these cemeteries and psych wards everywhere? These people didn't just wake up crazy or dead one day, obviously something more than they could handle was put on them, right?" she said while spinning around in her tight black dress, knowing it hugged her body perfectly in all the right places. "Look at you. You're a pastor but you're still human—you can't lie and act like you're not feeling me right now. You see exactly what I'm working with and you know you want it. Hell, I know you want it, and it's okay."

The prominent pastor was at a loss for words. He had no idea how the conversation had taken such a sudden turn—his eyes slowly began undressing her from head to toe. "I can't do it, it's not right," he said unconvincingly.

"Obviously looking at all this body is more than you can handle right now, right?" she said seductively, while moving closer. "C'mon, daddy, stop resisting. I've seen you look at me out the corner of your eye—don't act like you don't want none of this young pussy. It's hot, sweet and ready for you. It's real wet too, daddy. I'm sure God will understand if you got you a piece."

Before Pastor Armstrong could say a word, Erica was standing between his legs sucking his bottom lip before sticking her sweet tongue inside his mouth. "Mmm," she moaned as he sucked her tongue, cuffing her well-endowed backside with his massive hands. He wanted to sleep with her since the day she set foot inside his office, but he knew it was wrong in the eyes of God.

"Can I suck your dick?" she said suddenly as she reached down, grabbing the hard bulge in his pants.

Pastor Armstrong nearly lost it when she grabbed his erection. It took everything inside him to control himself.

"Oooh, my pussy is so wet," Erica said seductively as she continued to stroke his phallus through his thin slacks. "I know you want me, daddy, so

I'ma lean over your desk so you can fuck me from the back. Fuck me hard too, daddy."

The pastor's inner demons began to emerge and became much too powerful for him to fight off. He knew it was too late for him to turn back, so he let down his guard, succumbing to his desires.

The pastor leapt to his feet, locked his office door, then gave his young accountant what he thought she wanted. Instead of bending her over his desk like she suggested, he gently laid her down across his huge desk, gapped her legs open, pulled her panties aside, then buried his face in between her legs. He licked, kissed and sucked on her engorged clitoris like he was scarfing down a piece of chocolate cake topped with strawberry ice cream—he licked her clit-ring eagerly, aggressively and repeatedly, and continued to do so until she reached orgasm.

"Oh my god," Erica screamed with her pelvis rocking back and forth, her legs shaking as juice oozed from her pulsating hole. "I need you to give me that dick now. I need you to write your name in it, daddy."

"Not now," he said as he came to a halt, thinking he'd heard a noise but wasn't sure. "Get up and straighten out your clothes."

Erica did as she was told. She couldn't shake the thought of how well he'd sucked her pussy, he was even better at it than old man Charlie.

"Thank god nobody came to my office," he said when he realized the coast was clear. He used his handkerchief to wipe his mouth before looking at the teen who was already staring at him. "You can't mention this to anyone!"

"I won't," Erica said with a sly smile. "This will be me and daddy's dirty little secret. No one else will ever know."

Before Erica left his office, Pastor Armstrong slipped her a small yellow envelope containing one of the members' tithes—she assumed it was a gift to secure her silence, she also knew it was the beginning of something that would get worse. Much worse.

As soon as the over-developed teen left his office, Pastor Armstrong fell to his knees in the center of his office floor, and repented to God, begging for his forgiveness.

CHAPTER 8

Larry Kokane emerged immediately from the doorway of the main office of the J and J apartments when he saw the beautifully shaped woman exit her vehicle. He knew he'd never seen her or her vehicle before, but since he had an uncontrollable nature of being nosy, he made it his business to acquaint himself with her.

He approached her with caution, eyes fixated on her delicious looking thighs and rounded hips, which were accentuated by white thong straps that rose above her hip-hugging low-rider jeans, accompanied by a midriff top that exposed her chiseled torso. "Hello, good-lookin'," he said smoothly, looking suspicious as if he was up to no good. "I've never seen you in this area before so I assume you must be looking for me?" He hoped his sarcasm and good sense of humor would reel her in.

The woman noticed him heading in her direction immediately after he left the doorway and was silently hoping that she wasn't his target. She wasn't the slightest bit interested in him, nor the ill-fitting peach colored slacks he wore, so she tried to let him down as easily as possible. "No, I'm just here to see a friend," she said smiling, hoping he wouldn't continue wasting her precious time.

"Lucky friend," he said with his eyes bucked while staring her up and down, making her uncomfortable. "Whoever he is he's a lucky man."

"Thank you but it's a she," the woman said while easing away, hoping the man would take the hint and back off.

Larry watched as she walked away but was struggling to take his eyes off her banging body. *Goddam* he thought to himself as her ass cheeks jiggled from side to side. The scent of her sweet-smelling perfume continued to linger inside his nostrils—her round ass appeared to smell just as sweet. *Oh my goodness! Whoever is gettin' that is lucky as hell* he thought to himself as he hastily headed back toward the front office.

The woman approached the door to apartment 7 and was still looking behind her as she knocked with her key.

"Just a minute, I'm coming," Erica said while approaching the door. When she pulled it open and saw Danielle standing there, she found herself having to do a double take. "Dang, girl, you look good. I see you finally made your way over here."

"Yeah, ma, I told you I was coming," Danielle said as she stepped inside, surveying the front room of Erica's apartment. "This ain't bad, ma. I've never been inside one of these units before, but judging from the outside, I honestly didn't expect it to look this good."

Erica laughed as she closed the front door, twisting the locks as she stared at the backside of her new friend. Up to that point, the two women had mostly talked on the phone but had never seen each other outside the church— Erica had no idea that her friend/co-worker looked so good outside of her overalls. "I felt the same way when I first saw it. I done fucked around and fell in love with it now though."

"You seem excited; I'm happy for you," Danielle told her.

"Girl, I love having my own spot. It ain't nothin' in the world that's better than having your own shit."

"You got that right," Danielle said. "You should have seen me when I finally got my house. All I wanted to do was run around naked."

"I know what you mean," said Erica as she envisioned her co-worker running around naked. To her, Danielle was definitely an attractive woman—about a ten and a half on a scale from one to ten, but the teen didn't feel a sexual connection. "I'm not on that level yet, but hopefully one day. I know it has to feel good having your own house."

"It's small but it's mine," Danielle told her. "It took a long time to get, but with God's help, I finally got it."

"Girl, go ahead and have a seat," Erica said in joyous voice. "Can I get you something to eat or drink?"

"I'm cool, ma, thank you. I ate before I left home."

"I'm trying to practice being a good host. I have to get used to it. Besides you, ain't nobody else been over here but my moms and Pastor Armstrong. His old ass stay coming over here," Erica said with a giggle. "It's cool though. Lord knows I wouldn't be here if it wasn't for him."

Danielle's eyes were suddenly locked on Erica. She wondered if Mrs. Armstrong was right about her suspicions, so she decided to go ahead and be a little nosy. "Maybe he thinks he has a shot at getting a piece of that sweet chocolate?" she said with her brows raised. "You know them old men have always liked them some young girls."

"You know it ain't like that," Erica responded. "He's just a good man with a good heart. If it wasn't for him, I don't know where I'd be right now."

"Probably still at ya mama's house," Danielle said, raising her eyebrows again.

"Or on the street," added Erica. "A shelter or lockup or somewhere."

"Ain't none of that shit good," Danielle sighed. "That's good he cared enough to get you your own place, preventing you and Sister Willa from coming to blows."

Erica smiled as she pivoted her feet and began throwing punches as if she were boxing. "I'm so glad I didn't have to put these hands on that old lady. I'd really be in lockup then; I'm young but I ain't no pushover," she laughed.

"Y'all definitely didn't need that," Danielle said as she imagined the two women going toe-to-toe. "She hasn't said nothin' crazy to you at the church, has she?"

"I wish she would," Erica said, frowning. "If she do, we gon' fuck around and tear that church up."

Danielle burst out laughing as Erica began shadowboxing again. She was still curious about her new friend's relationship with Pastor Armstrong and was not quite ready to change the subject. "I hope it never come to that, but if she thinks her husband has something going with you, she just might want to see what you know from the shoulders. I mean, he is the pastor of

Real Love Baptist Church, that fool might be trying to love on somebody for real."

"Has he ever tried anything with you?" Erica asked while looking her in the eye.

"Hell no!" Danielle griped. "You know I don't do dudes, ma."

"That don't mean shit. That doesn't mean they don't be trying to do you," replied the teen. "I'm sure he didn't know that when he first saw you, so did it ever seem like he was trying to hit on you?"

"No."

"Okay then, that's all I'm saying," Erica said with emphasis. "I've done girls and dudes, but I haven't done him, nor do I want to," she continued. "I don't want no old broke dick or no saggy tea-bag balls hanging nowhere around me. That's not the shit that turns me on."

Danielle chuckled, then said, "I know that's right."

"Girl, look how fine you are," Erica said while eyeing her closely. "I had no idea you had this much body 'cause you're always wearing those damn overalls/coveralls, or whatever they are."

"Thank you," Danielle said, blushing.

"I said that to say this: Pastor Armstrong was younger when he met you. If he didn't want you as fine as you are, you know damn well he don't want me."

"I was somethin' else back then too," Danielle said. "I had ran away from home when I jumped on a bus and came to Vegas. I didn't know nothin' about this town when I got here, so I got into all kinds of mess just trying to eat."

"What kind of mess?"

"Stealing…robbing…burglarizing," Danielle told her. "You name it, I did it."

"How did you meet Pastor Armstrong?"

"I got caught stealing from a store one time and was placed in juvenile hall. I ended up befriending one of the women who worked there, who happened to be a member of the church at the time. Anyway, she asked Pastor Armstrong to come get me out once she learned I had no family out here. He came down, took guardianship over me and they released me to him, and, as they say, the rest is history."

"So, you stayed with them too?"

"No, I lived with the lady that worked at juvenile until she got tired of my shit and kicked me out. That's when Pastor Armstrong gave me my job at the church. Things began to turn around for me after that."

"So, you wouldn't be where you are without his help either?"

"Not even close," Danielle said. "I was able to keep a weekly with the money I made at the church until I was eventually able to save enough to get my own apartment." She'd also gotten assistance from Pastor Armstrong when she got her house, but she didn't feel like it was necessary to mention it to Erica. It crossed her mind to tell the teen about the visit she'd gotten from Mrs. Armstrong a couple of days prior, but she decided against it—she concluded Mrs. Armstrong was just paranoid. Danielle was convinced that

Erica was being truthful about her and the pastor, so she didn't feel the need to share his wife's suspicions.

"Girl, are you sure I can't get you no Kool-Aid or nothin'?"

"Nah, ma. I'm cool," Danielle said before grinning. She couldn't remember the last time she'd been offered Kool-Aid, or the last time she'd drank it—the offer alone was an instant turn-off, a blatant reminder of how young minded her friend really was. One minute she came across like a mature adult, and the next she acted as though she could be tamed with candy. "Alright, ma, I'ma go ahead and get out of here. I just wanted to get a look at your new place. I hope it turns out to be a sanctuary for you."

"It already is," the teen said with excitement.

"That's good, ma. All you gotta do now is get a car."

"He said he's gonna get me one, but first I gotta get my driver's license."

"Oh, so y'all done already talked about it?"

"Of course," Erica said, smiling. "You're not the only one who knows how to handle business."

"Gon' girl, get your pimp on then," Danielle laughed while giving her a high-five. "Now something like that might make me go against the grain; a sugar daddy is the only kind of man who might get some of this, especially right now. Just make sure Pastor Armstrong doesn't have his sights on you like that."

Erica smiled as she nodded her head. She didn't understand why Danielle couldn't seem to get off the subject, she wondered if her friend was hiding something?

"Look at you," Danielle continued. "That lil' thang you got down there is probably hot as hell, it'll probably catch on fire if you threw it up in the air," she said, fishing for answers.

"Girl, you crazy," Erica said as she opened the door, more ready than ever for Danielle to leave.

Danielle hoisted her bag over her shoulder, then stopped at the door and gave Erica a hug. The two women had both slept with their share of the same sex, but they didn't feel that kind of attraction toward each other.

Pastor Buddy Armstrong was just about to turn into the parking lot of the rundown apartments when he saw Danielle coming out of Erica's unit. He was a true believer of keeping his personal life separate from the church, so to avoid being seen, he kept going straight with the rest of the traffic, but double-backed to Erica's apartment a few minutes later.

He parked his car directly in front of her apartment, the same spot where Danielle had parked, and was greeted at the door with a warm embrace.

"Hey, handsome," Erica said, brandishing a huge grin.

"I take it you missed me today?" Pastor Armstrong said as he placed his hand on the small of her back, his other hand fumbling to close the door.

"You know I did," Erica said before kissing him on the lips.

The pastor immediately jerked away from her, slamming the door shut before barking at her. "Don't be kissing me with the door open, stupid," he said angrily. "Next time wait until the door is shut."

"Dang, I'm sorry," she said surprised, not understanding his anger. "Why are we hiding anyway when we're both grown? Your wife isn't here, and it's no one else's business what you and I do."

"Don't be stupid, young lady," he said bluntly. "You know darn well it isn't right what you and I are doing, and being seventeen doesn't make you grown."

"Apparently I'm grown enough for you," she stated bluntly.

Pastor Armstrong gave her an evil stare, wondering if he should stop while he was ahead?

"It might not be right to the rest of the world, but it's right for us if it's what we wanna do," the teen continued. "I don't give a damn what anyone else thinks, so come here daddy and sit next to mommy, I've been waiting for you to come by all day."

Pastor Armstrong did as his young mistress suggested. He sat on the couch and got comfortable.

Erica immediately swung her leg over his body then straddled his lap, locked her arms behind his neck, and began kissing him where she'd left off. "Mmmm," she moaned seductively as he sucked her tongue and bottom lip simultaneously before placing his large hand between her legs from the back. Erica buried her face between his neck and shoulder as he rubbed her crotch from the rear. It became a little too much for her, so she forced herself to climb from his lap.

She kneeled on the floor in front of him, a position she was comfortable and very familiar with, it made her feel like she was powerful and in control. She knew he was anticipating what she was about to do, so it wasn't a surprise when his erection leaped out at her immediately after she unbuckled and unzipped his pants. She took the entire length of his shaft inside her mouth, letting it slide down her throat, then sucked his balls inside her mouth as well.

"Oooh, Lord...Jesus!" he said as he wiggled beneath her.

Erica bobbed her head up and down his thick shaft before using her tongue ring to tease the head.

"My goodness," he said as he watched her devour his manhood. No woman had ever taken him entirely inside her mouth before, so he was really impressed by his young lover's skills.

"You like that?" she said when she came up for air. Her long tongue swirled slowly around the tip of his dick, then she took him inside her mouth again.

"I love it," he said while gasping, then sprawled out his legs to get more comfortable. He had never received oral sex from a woman wearing a tongue ring before, but he knew it was something he could easily get hooked on. "Suck it, Erica. Oooh, suck it!" he said as he grabbed the back of her head, pushing her mouth downward as far as it would go.

The teen remembered how good he'd eaten her pussy at the church, so she wanted to return the favor by making him come. She wondered if his wife's mouth was as skilled as hers, or if she even serviced him this way, but whatever the case, her mind was already set on giving him the best head he'd ever received.

Pastor Armstrong's buttocks began to stiffen. He tried his best to retain himself, but deep groans escaped his throat as he shot his load.

Erica used her long-wet tongue to lap up every drop, then raised her lips to his, sticking her tongue in his mouth. They kissed each other with electrifying passion; tasting each other's tongue endlessly before having intercourse for the first time.

Pastor Armstrong gave it everything he had before removing his dick from Erica's sauna-like vagina, shooting a thick load of cum all over her stomach.

He knew his fine teenage lover wasn't done yet, so he took his time climbing from between her legs before lying beside her on the hardwood floor, immediately wrapping his lips around her cocoa-colored nipple, sucking it thoroughly and firmly while rubbing her swollen clitoris with his middle finger.

Moments later she was moaning and squirting simultaneously before rolling onto her side, snuggling beside him.

Pastor Armstrong wrapped his arm around her, listening to her breathe, and then sprung the question that had been poking at him. "Why was Danielle over here?"

"How you know that?" she retorted immediately. "You got somebody spying on me or something?"

"Just answer the question," he said sharply.

"She just wanted to see my new apartment."

"I thought I said not to have any company!"

"Dang, I didn't know it was that serious."

Pastor Armstrong didn't respond, but his anger was apparent. He looked at the teen as if he wanted to kill her, the softness she usually saw in his eyes were no longer there.

"I didn't think it was a big deal since we work together. I just wanted her to see my new place. I'm sorry, daddy."

"Does she know anything about us?"

"She don't know shit," Erica said with emphasis—she cussed intentionally hoping it would get him to change the subject.

"Did she ask any questions?"

"No, daddy," she lied quickly. "I'm telling you she doesn't know nothin' so stop worrying. I know how to keep my business to myself."

"Make sure you keep it that way, okay," he said while peering at her. "I'm only your pastor if anyone asks. Nothing else."

"You're my boss."

"Yeah, but you know what I mean."

"I know, but ain't nobody ask me nothin'," Erica said trying to cheer him up. "Everybody is too busy worrying about their own business, ain't nobody got time to be worrying about mine."

Pastor Armstrong pushed his concerns aside as he leaned forward and kissed her neck. He began rubbing and squeezing her thigh and buttocks, momentarily he was ready to go again. "Your body is so soft."

"Have you ever done anything with Danielle?" Erica asked suddenly when she felt his hand slide between her legs.

"Heaven's no," he shot back. "Why would you ask that?"

"I'm just asking," Erica said softly. She then reached down and wrapped her hand around his semi-erect penis. She felt it getting bigger and harder as she held it in her hand. The minute she thought he was fully erect, she opened her legs wide and placed him inside her, then raised her legs in the air and locked her ankles behind his neck—her eyes shut when he thrust himself forward.

She watched his facial expressions as he made love to her, still wondering if him and Danielle had ever done anything?

CHAPTER 9

Willa Armstrong was not having it. She laid fully awake on her side of the bed, back facing her husband, with a large pillow wedged snugly between her buttocks and his larger than life body. She kept him at bay with a sharp elbow when he made a half-hearted attempt to hold her from behind.

"Honey, why are you always acting like this?" he said with frustration in his voice, wondering why she wasn't as submissive as she once was. "We used to make love all the time, now I'm lucky if we do it twice a year."

"What time did you come home last night, or should I say this morning?" she asked as she twisted her neck awkwardly to look at him.

"Around eleven or twelve. Why?"

"More like one or two," she said, correcting what she knew was a blatant lie. "Now why would a respected pastor be out by himself at that time of morning, or was there someone with you keeping you company?"

"C'mon now, honey, don't start that," he said in a whiny voice. "Why would you ask me something like that, who else could I have possibly been with?"

"I don't know you tell me," she said while rolling her eyes.

"I was out riding around, thinking about how much you mean to me, trying to figure out what we need to do to get our marriage back on track."

Willa Armstrong remained quiet. Her husband's words penetrated her lonely heart—she responded by running her hand slowly up and down his leg, causing something to stir deep inside herself. She, too, wanted things to get back to how they once were—she was tired of feeling as though she was gradually losing her husband. Their relationship meant the world to her, and she wanted to do whatever it took to keep it together, even if it meant she had to compromise.

"I love you, sweetheart, and I miss you," he stated softly. He kissed her gently on the ear, then pulled the pillow from between their bodies.

"I love and miss you too," she whispered without turning around. Instead, she reached back, found his semi-erect penis and carefully pulled it through the pee-hole of his boxers, then closed her hand around it and began stroking it gently.

Pastor Armstrong closed his eyes and enjoyed his wife's touch. The deep passion within him began to boil like an active volcano; he immediately allowed his hand to roam all over her well-endowed backside, squeezing and caressing every inch of it as she continued to stroke his penis with her delicate hand. The plumpness of her well-defined assets got the best of him, in no time, he was fully erect and ready for business.

UNGODLY

He couldn't recall the last time he and his wife had been intimate, so he was really excited about the treat he was about to receive—he hoped it was the moment that would turn things around.

He stared at her massive backside after hiking her gown up around her waist, caressed it with his hand, then rolled her onto her stomach, pulling down her panties.

"Take your time, baby, there's no need to rush," she said with a great deal of calmness.

"I miss you so much," he said as he yanked down his boxers, eyes fixated on the mounds of his wife's beautifully shaped ass. He was surprised when she reached back with both hands to spread her goodies apart, he didn't hesitate to mount her from behind and began pounding.

"Oooh, Buddy, slow down—don't rush," she said as she braced herself.

Her husband was too focused to say anything. He forcefully thrust his hips forward again and again, causing her head to hit the headboard repeatedly as she thrust back her pelvis, matching his rhythm.

"Yes, baby, get this pussy!" she said between moans before burying her face inside a pillow. She continued to hold her ass cheeks open for him, allowing him to plunge in as deep as he possibly could. He went deeper and deeper with every stroke.

"Oooh, baby, I like how you got it spread open for me," he said as he continued to pound her hard from the back.

"Get your pussy, baby…get it!" Mrs. Armstrong yelled. "Oh my god, baby, I love how that big juicy dick feels inside this wet pussy." It had been so long since the two had gotten this down and dirty, Mrs. Armstrong forgot it could be so good.

Pastor Armstrong seemed to think he'd died and went to heaven as he fervently continued to thrust his hips forward. It had been at least a decade since he'd heard her speak so vulgarly, hearing it spiel from her lips turned him on even more. "You miss this dick don't you, bitch?" he said without thinking, but continued to plunge in and out of her.

Beads of sweat dripped profusely from his face and forehead falling onto her back as his thrusts continued to get more intense. Suddenly, his entire body began to stiffen, he nearly blacked out when he came inside of her.

Mrs. Armstrong rolled over and cradled her husband's head between her bosom and shoulder, using her hand to wipe sweat from his forehead as he lay panting, she could only smile as she pressed her face against his.

In the nearly four decades they'd been together, she couldn't remember a time when he gave her that kind of affection—for reasons unknown to her, his history of being gentle with her had turned into raw passion. "That was good, baby. You put it down!" she said smiling, the inside of her vagina still flowing remnant juices while throbbing. "I love you so much, baby."

"I love you, too," he said softly before he rolled off of her body and laid beside her. He felt her warm soft lips press lightly against his, but he was simply too exhausted to reciprocate.

UNGODLY

He was extremely grateful for the intimate moment he'd just shared with his wife, but he couldn't stop Erica from entering his mind. They had just made love the evening before, but already, he was beginning to miss her terribly.

For the most part, the day started off well for Mrs. Armstrong. She strolled down the aisle of Real Love Baptist Church, swaying her wide hips back and forth as she brandished a huge grin while approaching the exit. "Well, good morning, Miss Danielle and Miss Erica," she said in her most pleasant voice.

"Good morning," they said in unison before she made her departure.

The few staff members who remained at the church were in high spirits as they raced to put finishing touches on a deacon's wedding that was scheduled to take place later that afternoon. It took them nearly two days to set up for it.

Danielle had just finished vacuuming every nook and cranny in the main part of the church. She and Erica stood chatting inside the janitor's closet, both equally surprised by the unusual greeting. "I understand why she spoke to me, but I really don't get why she spoke to you," Danielle said in a low voice.

"She fucked me up with that too," Erica whispered before peeking outside the janitor's closet, making sure no one else was in earshot. "I don't know what's up with that. Maybe the good lord done got to her or something," she joked.

"It's possible," Danielle uttered. "Or maybe the pastor gave her some of that pipe last night?"

"She is his wife so it's possible," Erica said as she shrugged her shoulders, feeling a tinge of jealousy as she thought about it.

"Well, at least she's being nice to you. It's a lot better than her turning her nose up at you," Danielle laughed as she came out of the closet, flicking off the light.

"That's true," Erica said without smiling. "We'll see how long it lasts though. I personally think it's all a front."

"I wouldn't doubt it," Danielle told her. "They say people in the church be the fakest ones."

"Sounds right to me," the teen said.

The main part of the church was decorated for the wedding, so they did their best to stay out of the way. Danielle and Erica looked up simultaneously when they heard what sounded like loose change, it was the maintenance girl Ne-Ne rounding the corner; she seemed to be making a beeline to the pastor's office.

"She's always walking around here making all that damn noise," Danielle said with a giggle.

"She must have a key to every door in the city on that key ring? I know damn well this church don't have that many locks."

"I wonder why she goes to his office so much, and she only goes when no one else is around," Danielle said, being messy on purpose.

"I don't know," said Erica. "I don't think she's the pastor's type. Shit, I don't think she's anyone's type."

"I don't know about that, ma. One day I went to his office to tell him something and that bitch was crawling from underneath his desk."

"You bullshittin'…are you serious?" Erica said, quizzically.

"As a heart attack, you know I wouldn't play about something like that."

"Maybe something was under there that needed to be fixed," she joked.

"Like what, his dick?"

"Was he sitting at his desk when she came from under it?"

"Hell yeah, he was sitting there," Danielle said. "That bitch did have that tool belt on though, so I guess she could have been under there fixing something. It aint no tellin'."

Erica didn't laugh at her co-worker's joke. She personally didn't find any humor in it, plus Danielle's laughing only ticked her off more.

As far as Erica was concerned, in her mind, Pastor Buddy Armstrong was her new man, and regardless of their age difference, she felt herself falling in love with him. "Fuck that, I'm going in there," she said as she headed toward his office, and found herself wondering if Danielle knew about her and the pastor?

"Uh-uh, ma, don't do that!" Danielle warned, remembering how upset he'd gotten the time she walked in on him. "I'm telling you, ma, that's a good way to get fired."

"I don't care, I'm going in," Erica said without turning around. As soon as she got past the choir stand, the pastor and Ne-Ne came through the door.

"I gotta make a quick run to the supply store," he said while looking at Erica. "It shouldn't take no more than a few minutes. Y'all take care of the church until I get back."

"Alright," Erica said before glancing back at Danielle, who was still standing near the back of the church.

Pastor Armstrong dug into his pocket and removed his car keys before walking in the direction where Danielle was standing, Ne-Ne quickly pushed off in the opposite direction.

The teen felt so relieved when she learned Danielle's assumptions were wrong. She was smiling from ear to ear as she headed towards her.

CHAPTER 10

T he J and J apartment manager thought he was dressed to kill when he left his apartment just after sunset. He had a date with a middle-aged woman he met at a carwash two weeks prior, his only agenda was to sleep with her. They talked on the phone nearly every day since the day they met, but because of her hectic work schedule as a supervisor for the Clark County School District—they couldn't get together until time permitted.

During one of their phone conversations, they discovered that they both had a thing for seafood, so for their first date, they agreed to meet at Red Lobster for some delicious deep-fried catfish.

Larry Kokane was a prima donna; a self-proclaimed mack from way back, who couldn't seem to let go of the 1970's. He was also a hopeless romantic who still believed in flowers and candy, picnics in the park, walking and holding hands, candlelight dinners and surprising each other with expensive gifts—he refused to believe that chivalry was dead.

He looked into his rear-view mirror before pulling his red and white Cadillac Eldorado into the parking lot of a jewelers, just off the Strip. He planned to purchase his new friend Valarie a special gift. Not one that was too expensive, but he wanted it to be better than flowers and candy. His goal was to make his second impression better than his first—something that the majority of people thought was impossible, but the old-school player, knew better.

He pulled the door open and entered the jewelry store, instantly noticing a woman's well-endowed backside as she leaned over a glass encasement, viewing a pallet of gold men's watches, holding a perfect doggy-style form. *Goddam* he said to himself as he popped a mint inside his mouth, heading in her direction.

The bell from the door opening caught the woman's attention—she turned her head just in time to catch him gazing at her. "Larry, is that you?" she said as she turned toward him.

"You know it, the one and only," he said as he got closer. "How you doin', Willa?"

"I'm fine," she said, smiling.

"I didn't ask how you look, I asked how you doin'?" he said smoothly.

"I see you're still crazy," she said, blushing. "It's been a long time, hasn't it?"

"Too long, but you still look the same," he shot back while extending his arms. "You look good, girl."

"You're still lookin' pretty decent yourself," she said as she hugged him with one arm, noticing he still dressed the same as he did when they were dating.

"The watches you're checking out look pretty expensive. Who's the lucky man?" he asked nosily.

"My husband of course, who else would it be?" she said with emphasis. "I'ma get him a watch, it's been a while since I've given him something new."

"You and Buddy are still together, huh?" he asked, pretending not to know.

"Yep, still together."

"Good for y'all," he said, wishing he could still get in her panties, especially after seeing how good she still looked. "I'm glad to hear that man is doing right by you."

"He is, thank god," she said, smiling. "What about you, did you ever get married?"

"Nah, not yet," he said as he shook his head. "Not because I don't want to, but when I do decide to do it, I want it to be right, and for the right reasons."

"That's incredible to hear, Larry. I'm proud of you."

"Well, thank you, Miss Willa," he said earnestly. "I believe I just met my wife though, I'm in here now to buy her a lil somethin'-somethin'."

"Ooh, gon' with your bad self," she said with her hand on her hip. "I wish you and whoever she is the best. If you're still the womanizer you used to be, I'm sure you got other choices on standby."

"I'm not like that no more, Willa. Those days are over with. Now that I see you, I'm starting to wish I had kept you."

"Oh no, let's not bring up the past," she frowned. "Look at you. Men ain't about nothin'. I thought you just said you think you found your wife?"

"That's true, but I still can't get over how good you look," he said as he stepped back, giving her a onceover. "My bad, baby. I don't mean no disrespect."

"None taken," she told him, but was turned off and offended by his choice of words. She could see that he was still into playing games, which was the one thing she didn't have patience for. "I hate to cut this conversation short, Larry, but I really do need to get out of here. It's real good seeing you again, though. Let's exchange phone numbers so we can keep in touch."

"I was just about to suggest the same thing," he said, brandishing a huge grin.

The two exchanged phone numbers and parted ways, but not before giving each other another hug.

Larry Kokane purchased a fourteen-karat gold charm bracelet for his friend Valarie. He spent a lot more on it than he originally intended, but he knew it was an investment that was well worth it.

His feelings were confirmed when he sat across from his new prospect at Red Lobster. She was more beautiful than she was the first time he'd seen her; her elegance and poise was intoxicating.

"I can't believe you're late for our first date," she said with disappointment in her voice.

"Only by a few minutes, honey. We didn't miss out on nothin', did we?"

"It doesn't matter, sweetheart, this is still our first date," she said again. "The one we've been planning for two weeks now. The very least you could have done was be on time."

Larry looked at Valarie with sympathy in his eyes. His only plan was to bring her happiness, the last thing he wanted to do was hurt her feelings. "I'm sorry, baby. I didn't intend to be late for our first date, but I didn't think it would be gentlemen-like to show up empty handed, so I stopped and bought you a little something," he said as he reached into his pocket, producing a plastic bag that contained a box.

The beautiful Valarie was at a loss for words.

She raised both of her hands to cover her mouth. She couldn't believe he had actually bought her a gift. "Awww, you didn't have to do that."

Larry extracted the small box from inside the bag, sat it on the table just inches away from her, then pulled the lid off and watched her response. "Go ahead, baby, it's for you," he said while staring at her.

"Thank you so much, Larry...it's beautiful," she said while inspecting it. "Buying me dinner was sufficient enough, you didn't have to buy me a gift, baby."

"I did it because I wanted to," he said calmly. "I wanted you to know how special and wonderful I think you are."

"Thank you, Larry. Thank you so much," she said as tears welled in her eyes. "I happen to think you're special, too."

"Hold on. A minute ago you were about to put your fist down my throat for being late, now all of a sudden you think I'm special?" he joked.

"You can't be bringing up the past—that's old stuff," she said, smiling. "Look forward and focus on where you're going, not where you've been."

"I gotta give it to you, that's pretty smooth," he said, laughing.

"Nah, baby, I didn't mean to snap at you for being late. I'm sorry, now can you please help me put my bracelet on?" she said with a grin.

He took the sparkling gold bracelet from her hand, fastening it around her wrist, then secured the safety clamp to insure it wouldn't come off. "Looks great on you," he said as he stared at it.

"Thank you, it feels good. It feels right."

"Being with you feels right," he said, still holding her hand, staring down at her wrist. "You're such a beautiful woman, Valarie. I think the bracelet should be thanking you."

"Thanking me. Why?"

"Because you make it look good. Instead of it complementing you, you complement it."

"Awww, thank you. You're so crazy," she said, smiling.

They continued to flirt back and forth while enjoying their catfish dinner before going back to her place to watch a movie.

CHAPTER 11

Two months after Erica moved into her new apartment she had a 2016 Chevy Malibu to go with it. Pastor Armstrong made life much easier for her. Not only was she grateful for having him, but they seemed to grow closer with each day that passed.

The expression *better late than never* was resonating to her more than ever before. Her life had been in shambles for more than seventeen years, now that all the pieces of the puzzle were falling into place, she was really enjoying the great things God was doing for her.

The teen sat on the couch in her living room, listening intently to her mom, who was making it very clear how upset she was.

"Erica, why in the hell are you calling this man daddy?" she said with a concerned look on her face, shocked by her daughter's choice of words. "He's not your daddy, he's our pastor." Lisa had never heard her daughter call anyone daddy before, it troubled her to hear it roll so easily off her tongue.

"I know, mama. I misspoke," she said, trying to clean it up. "He's like the father I've never had but always wanted. I just be wanting him to know how much I appreciate him."

"You don't have to refer to him as daddy to show him your appreciation. Don't ever do that again. Not in front of me, him, or anyone else, do you understand?"

"It won't happen again. My bad," Erica said while looking down at the floor.

Lisa miles acted as though she didn't hear her daughter's apology—she continued to express how she felt about it. "It's not nice or appropriate for a young girl like you to be calling an older man daddy, especially when he's not your daddy or my husband," she said before pausing. "Pastor Armstrong has helped you a lot, and I appreciate him for that, but he's nothing more than a friend and the pastor of the church. I'm sure he already knows you appreciate him for being there for you, otherwise, he wouldn't keep helping you the way he do."

"I know, mama. I've already told you I misspoke."

"Well, don't do it again because it's not nice," her mom repeated.

Erica felt like a toddler who was once again living under her mother's roof instead of her own. She dreaded these kind of never-ending lectures, and she knew it was time to bring it to an end.

If there's any truth to the expression *practice makes perfect* then she became a professional at wiggling out from underneath her mother, especially when she got tired of hearing what she was saying. The same bait worked for her every time. She knew exactly what her mom liked, and not once had it failed to shut her up. "Mom, I'm glad you stopped by today. I got paid yesterday and I wanted to give you a few dollars."

"Oh yeah? What you got for me, baby?"

"Just a few dollars," Erica said as she leaned forward, grabbing her purse from the coffee table. "Enough to get you something to eat, and probably a new pair of pants and maybe a shirt."

"Okay," said Lisa.

Erica handed her mom a hundred dollars, counting it out with five twenty-dollar bills, but she knew her mom would only use it to buy drugs. She really didn't care how she'd choose to spend it; she was just glad to be able to do something for her, and to move her away from the subject of Pastor Armstrong.

"Thank you, baby. Mama love you so much," Lisa said as she neatly folded the bills, then stuffed them carefully inside her bra.

"I love you, too," said Erica. "Make sure you go get something to eat first."

"I will, baby, thank you. Mama gotta go now—I'll see you soon."

"Alright, mama, be careful out there," she said as she hugged her.

Lisa miles pulled the door open before turning to her daughter, then stood inside the doorway with her hand on her hip and spoke to her in all seriousness. "Erica, I had you...you didn't have me, okay? You can best believe I know what I'm doing out here in these streets. I don't need nobody telling me to be careful. You can best believe I got this! You just better be careful about how you address your pastor," she said as she pulled the door shut, not permitting her daughter a chance to reply.

But he is my daddy Erica said to herself as she locked the door. She grabbed an ice-cold beer from the refrigerator and drank it quickly, then made a beeline to her bedroom closet and pulled out an outfit, laying it neatly across the bed, then stripped down naked, preparing to take a shower.

Wednesdays were the slowest day of the week at Real Love Baptist Church. The usher board met for about an hour in the afternoon, choir rehearsal wouldn't take place until the evening, so the entire staff pretty much had the day off.

Pastor Armstrong showed up faithfully on a daily basis because he was one of two people who had keys to the church—the maintenance girl Ne-Ne was the other one.

On this particular Wednesday, no one other than Erica even bothered to show up, and she only showed up because the pastor requested it. Her initial plans were to meet up with her old friends Bubbles, Menace, and Dominique for a little get-together at Bubbles parents' apartment, but those plans obviously had to be put on hold. She was more than certain that there was going to be lots of smoking and drinking going on amongst her friends, because it always was, but she was more interested in going to show off her new car.

She watched Pastor Armstrong as he sat at his desk. He appeared to have something heavy on his mind—it was clear to her that he was in deep thought. "What's wrong, daddy?" she said in her softest voice, ignoring what her mom had just told her earlier. She walked around his desk, stood behind his chair and waited for him to acknowledge her.

"Nothing," he said while staring at the ceiling.

Erica placed her hands on his chest from the back and eased them toward his stomach as she leaned forward. "Talk to me, daddy. Tell me what's wrong," she said before kissing his neck and nibbling on his earlobe.

She saw his lack of response as an indicator that something was wrong, and if she hoped to find out what was troubling him, she knew she would first have to get him to speak.

She sucked his earlobe inside her mouth, slowly, gently, salaciously, then ran her warm-wet tongue all around the inside of his ear then slipped her hand inside his pants.

He gasped.

"Oh, you like that, huh?" she said as she continued fondling him, feeling his manhood spring to life inside her hand.

Erica removed her hand from inside his pants, hoisted her skirt up around her tiny waist, stared at him, and then turned around so he could get a good look at her. With her ample backside exposed, she bent over slightly to show off her thong, she then felt his large hand squeezing and caressing her ass cheek.

She became fully relaxed when she felt him kissing and sucking her right ass cheek while simultaneously squeezing the left side with his powerful hand.

The teen smiled as she leaned forward and rested her hands on the edge of his desk, giving him more access to her chocolate spread. "You like how this ass feel, don't you?" she said in a seductive voice. She could no longer fight the urge as he squeezed and sucked her ass cheeks; she spun around swiftly, kissed him passionately on the mouth, then kneeled on the floor in front of him.

"Please, Lord, forgive me," Pastor Armstrong whispered.

"Is this what you want?" Erica said as she unzipped his pants and pulled down his boxers, coming face-to-face with his swollen member. She placed the head of his dick delicately inside her mouth and felt his hand on the back of her head as he pushed her mouth down until it was at its base. She sucked his dick back and forth, in a deep-slow rhythm, then sped up the pace and continued sucking until she felt globs of sperm hitting the back of her throat. "Mmmm," she hummed softly as she continued to bob her head up and down. She then placed his limp penis back inside his pants before climbing from her knees as if nothing had happened.

Pastor Armstrong took a moment to catch his breath, then wheeled his chair to his desk, but remained seated.

"Are you gonna tell me what's on your mind or what?" Erica said with her hand on her hip.

Pastor Armstrong closed the large Bible that sat on his desk in front of him, then looked sadly at Erica, whose eyes were already locked on him. "I'm starting to think what we're doing is not a good idea anymore," he said in a low voice. "I feel so hypocritical sitting here. My guilty conscience is starting to eat away at me."

"But, daddy, I just sucked your dick; what are you talking about?"

"That's exactly what I'm talking about," he said, confused. He thought about her tongue-ring and how good it felt sliding up and down his swollen member. He knew that his teenage lover had him hooked, but he also knew how important it was for him to back away from her. "It's not good what we're doing, Erica. It's really been messing up my head lately."

"Oh, Lord," she said with a sigh. "I guess you got what you wanted so that's it, huh?"

"I love you, Erica, but I am a married man and a pastor for Christ's sake."

"What the hell does that have to do with anything, you knew all of that before we started messing around," she said with disappointment in her voice.

"I'm not saying it's your fault or blaming you for anything," Pastor Armstrong told her. "I'm a grown man and I should have known better. I just don't think our escapades should continue."

Erica moved toward the pastor, closed her hand around his, looked down while inching closer, causing his chair to recline, then placed his hand on the small of her back. "I love you too, daddy, and I don't want this to end."

He allowed his hand to stay where she'd placed it, then peered up at her with emotion-filled eyes. "What are you saying?"

"I'm in love with you, daddy, and I want us to be together. Let's just let it run its course and see what happens."

"What about my wife?"

"What about her?" the teen said coldly. "You're my only concern, it's up to you what you decide to do with her."

"I want to be with you, too," he said while giving her ass a squeeze. "I'll try not to worry too much about it; I just have to let go and let God."

Erica hesitated before replying. The expression was one that she had always been bothered by—it was one she had never been able to fathom. "How does somebody just let go and let God?" she frowned. "I don't even know how that's possible."

"I don't find it difficult to do at all," the pastor told her. "A lot of things are just out of our control, sometimes letting go is all we can do."

"Everything we do, we do on our own," she said adamantly. "Nothing will ever get done if we don't do it ourselves. If that's the case, lazy people who never do anything can say they're letting go and letting God as their excuse for being lazy. Would you be able to accept that as an answer if somebody constantly said that to you?"

It was times like these when her age was apparent, the teen was just too young to understand, and Pastor Armstrong didn't feel like going into detail about it. To him, it was neither controversial nor contradictory. At least one of the books in the Bible speaks about lazy people and the rewards for those who are doers, but while growing up he had always been told to let go and let God, he knew he was just repeating what had been instilled in him.

"Never thought of it like that. You might have a point," he said nonchalantly. "You're definitely wrong about one thing though. Nothing we do is on our own, God gives us the strength to do everything we do."

"If you say so," the teen retorted.

"And, as far as lazy people are concerned, a lot of people lack motivation because not everyone knows their purpose in life."

"Speaking of not knowing, I got one more question, and that'll be it."

"Shoot."

"You know how they say Jesus was omniscient?"

"Yes."

"How can that be true when the Bible clearly states that no one knows the day nor hour that God will return?"

Pastor Armstrong took a deep breath and nodded his head, trying his best to come up with an answer that would be comprehensible to her. "God is omniscient, not Jesus."

"But aren't they one?"

"They are——."

"So how can one know something and the other doesn't?"

"Young lady, in order to understand how it all works, you'll have to first understand——."

"I don't want to argue about it so let's leave it alone," she said as she cut him off.

"It blows my mind how you come up with this stuff. Where do all of these crazy questions and views come from?"

"I don't know," said Erica. "I guess I just have an inquiring mind. That's not a bad thing, is it?"

"Information is powerful, so it's always good to ask questions," he said.

The teen informed him that she'd seen her mom earlier that day and had given her a hundred dollars, and without her asking for it, he went inside the church's safe and reimbursed her. "I swear to god I don't know anyone else as nice as you."

"Somebody's gotta do it," he said while gazing at her.

The two talked for a few minutes before leaving his office, they both had other engagements they had to attend.

CHAPTER 12

The J and J apartments weren't strangers to police activity. The gateway to get inside the apartment complex was more comparable to an alley than a parking lot—local hoodlums liked to gather to socialize in flocks because they had a clear view of everyone who tried to approach, making it extremely difficult for law enforcement to make any arrests.

After dark it was a place where ex-felons and other low-life's liked to sell illegal products to a plethora of customers, whether it was guns, drugs, women or stolen goods—everything the criminals had was in high demand.

The Seven-Seas nightclub across the street provided a special shelter. With so many people constantly coming and going, whether in cars or on foot, it was sometimes difficult for law-enforcement to detect who was actually leaving the club after a long night of partying or leaving the apartments after engaging in some kind of illegal activities.

The apartment's next-to-nothing rent provided a safe haven for criminals to do their business in private, so the Las Vegas Metropolitan Police Department relied on the law-abiding residents who lived in the complex to keep an eye open for the apartments that had excessive traffic, or anything else that looked suspicious.

Larry Kokane watched intently through the blinds of the office while the police raided a corner apartment, whom he strongly suspected was selling some kind of illegal products. He rented the unit to a young couple only two weeks prior, but already, their apartment was a high-traffic area. The watchful office manager reported his suspicions to the authorities the day before, so he was very much aware that the calvary was coming.

He watched as the young couple was yanked from their apartment in handcuffs and thrown into separate patrol cars just minutes before a drug-sniffing K-9 was set loose inside their apartment, and in less than a minute, the dog sat on the floor inside the kitchen and barked continuously while looking back and forth between a drawer and his handler. Once the drawer was pulled open a large bag of pills, determined later to be the drug known as ecstasy was discovered, along with several plastic baggies of marijuana, a sandwich bag filled with methamphetamine, and a loaded 40 caliber pistol that was ready for business. "Good boy," the officer said as he patted the K-9's head.

The young couple was immediately whisked off to jail, which was a welcomed sight to the office manager.

He was just about to leave the office window when he saw Pastor Armstrong's car pull into the parking lot and park in front of Erica's apartment. He watched the good-for-nothing pastor exit his vehicle and do a quick survey of the area before approaching the teenager's apartment.

He witnessed a huge smile spread quickly across the teenager's face when she opened the front door and saw the pastor. She hugged him inside the doorway and received an unexpected affectionate smack on the backside when she turned around to let him inside. *Why is he smacking that young girl's ass?* He thought the gesture was very distasteful as he continued to stare, at a man everyone thought of as a pillar in the black community, but according to his actions, he was nothing more than a pedophile.

Larry Kokane suddenly remembered he had Willa Armstrong's phone number programmed in his phone, so he pulled it from his pocket and gave her a ring.

"Hello."

"Hey, Miss Willa, how you doin' this evening?" he said calmly, not sure if he was making the right decision. He knew that what the pastor was doing was wrong, but he didn't feel comfortable getting involved.

"I'm fine, Larry, how are you?"

"I'm makin' it," he said nervously.

"Well that's good. We all have to try to do that, don't we?"

"I don't think we have no other choice," he said as he loosened up.

"It's good to hear from you," she told him. "At least I know you didn't throw away my number."

"I wouldn't do that," he said smoothly. "I've thought about you a lot over the years. I nearly fainted when I saw you the other day. I still can't believe how good you look."

"Hush, Larry before you make me blush."

"I'm just tellin' you the truth, Miss Willa. You can't fault a man for being honest."

"I appreciate the compliment, Larry, but I'm still the same happily married woman that I was when you saw me the other day. I'm waiting for my husband to show up now, I got his dinner in the oven, waiting for him."

"…Well, that's sort of why I'm calling, Miss Willa."

"Is my husband ok?"

"Oh, I'm sure he's fine," replied the office manager. "Are you familiar with the J and J apartments on the corner of Lake Mead and H?"

"Across from Seven-Seas?"

"Those are the ones," he said before pausing. "I manage those apartments, Miss Willa. I see everything that goes on around here, and if you show up right now and go to apartment 7, you'll find your husband inside with a young lady."

"What!" she said with trembling in her voice, too frightened and embarrassed to elaborate further.

"Yep, I'm sorry, but that's where he's at," repeated the office manager. "He's been spending quite a bit of time with her lately. I could be wrong, but I don't think he has plans on coming home for dinner this evening."

"Larry, what are you talking about—what in God's name are you saying to me?"

"I just told you, Miss Willa. I'm sorry to be the bearer of bad news, but I think you should come over and see for yourself. I'd really appreciate it if you don't mention my name."

Mrs. Armstrong hung up the phone on him. He knew that she was more than likely simmering with anger, so he didn't bother with trying to call her back.

Larry peeked through the blinds once more to see if Pastor Armstrong's car was still parked in front of Erica's apartment. It was, and the one he'd bought her was parked next to it.

The office manager reached for his phone again, called a number he had on speed dial, it wasn't long before he heard a voice on the other end.

"Hellooo."

"Hey, sweetheart," he said smoothly.

"Oh, hi. I was just thinking about you, I'm glad you called."

"I've been thinking about you, too."

"Really?"

"Really," he said, smiling.

"Well, I've been thinking about you more," Valarie said in a sexy voice. "Are you still at work?"

"I am but I'm off the clock. I'm getting ready to walk out the door now," he said as he switched off the lights. "Actually, I was thinking about coming to see you."

"Come on, that'll be good," she said cheerfully. "I got somebody I want you to meet."

"Who?"

"The other man in my life—my son Chris."

"Oh, Chris."

"Yep, he's dying to meet you."

"Well, I guess I'm dying to meet him too then," he said sarcastically.

"His restaurant isn't far from the Strip, and he said he wants to cook something special for us."

"Sounds good," Larry said as he glanced at his watch after locking the door to the front office. "Are we going tonight?"

"Yeah, if you're down for it."

"Tonight's fine with me. I'm down with whatever you wanna do, my stomach is touching my back right now."

"Mine, too," she said, laughing. "Now we have an even better reason to go out there. Come to my place as soon as possible, I'll give him a call to let him know we're coming."

"Sounds good, baby, I'm looking forward to meeting him—how old is he again?"

"Thirty-one," said Valarie. "My baby's the owner and chef and takes great pride in everything he does."

"Let me take a quick shower and I'll be out there. I shouldn't be no more than thirty minutes."

"Alright, baby, I'll be waiting," she said before hanging up.

Larry Kokane rushed to his apartment to take a shower; he couldn't wait to be in his woman's presence.

UNGODLY

Ten minutes after receiving the disturbing phone call, Mrs. Willa Armstrong pulled into the parking lot of the J and J apartments and parked directly behind her husband's vehicle. She hopped out of her car and kept the ignition running, before going to apartment 7 as she was instructed. All kinds of wicked thoughts raced through her head as she stopped abruptly at the door—she didn't know if she was more upset with her husband or the female companion she was told he was with—she knocked on the door and waited for it to open.

The well-endowed teenager was half naked when she pulled the door open—she stood in the doorway wearing an evil smirk, as if she somehow knew Mrs. Armstrong was coming.

At first glance, Mrs. Armstrong had no reaction to Erica. She acted as though the teen was invisible, but her mouth fell to the floor when she saw her husband standing in the background, wearing only his boxers, eyes popping from their sockets as he stared at her. "So, this is where you be at, huh?" she said, appearing not to be angry, but was using all the strength she could muster to contain herself.

"Ba-baby, I can explain," he stuttered.

Mrs. Armstrong coolly turned around and walked back to her car. She was not at all interested in hearing his explanation—she knew their marriage was over with.

Pastor Armstrong was shocked as he gazed at Erica. The day he dreaded had finally arrived, but he was still shocked that he'd been caught.

He ran out of Erica's apartment wearing only his boxers, hoping to catch up with his wife, but was met by the brightness of her tail lights as she sped out of the parking lot.

He stopped in his tracks. He had no idea what to do next.

CHAPTER 13

It can be difficult at times trying to understand the complexities of life. One minute a person can be on top of the world, and the next they can be at the bottom of the barrel.

No matter how famous or important a person may be, there's just no escaping life's ups and downs. Whatever trial or tribulation one encounters in life, it's how one chooses to deal with it that will determine who stays down or who climbs back up.

Pastor Buddy Armstrong found himself battling some serious issues. At times he wasn't sure whether he was coming or going as he struggled to maintain his social standing, as well as his pastorship at Real Love Baptist Church.

Many of his longtime followers immediately turned their back on him when they learned of his infidelity to Willa, of whom they thought was adorable—they suddenly left the church without warning.

At first, he tried to act like he didn't know why she skipped out, but through social media posts, and text messages, his wife revealed to several members of the congregation, the real reason she decided to leave the church.

There was no denying the fact that she'd caught him fooling around with another woman, but fortunately for him, she didn't reveal to anyone who the culprit was, which unfortunately, enabled him and Erica to continue their despicable relations.

In public, as well as in the presence of friends, Pastor Armstrong pretended as though everything was fine, but behind closed doors, he was a total wreck. Although he preached it on several occasions, the disgraced pastor didn't know the first thing about sacrifice. He was unbelievably avarice and refused to let his wife or his young lover go—he simply wanted to have his cake and eat it too.

A couple of weeks passed since he was caught with his pants down inside Erica's apartment, and it troubled him, that already Mrs. Armstrong had filed for divorce. She went out and found a pro-bono attorney, who didn't hesitate to get the proceedings started, especially after she told him what had transpired.

For the first time in thirty-eight years, Mr. and Mrs. Armstrong resided under the same roof, but in two separate bedrooms—their physical contact was nonexistent. No sex. No hugs. No kisses. Nothing. Mrs. Armstrong decided it was best to keep it that way, so she totally ignored him when they were in each other's presence.

He on the other hand, hoped she would eventually come around, because he was very much still in love with her. It ate away at his soul to be treated like he was invisible; his out-of-control ego didn't allow him to take it lightly.

UNGODLY

Pastor Armstrong tried to carry on as if everything was ok, but it wasn't. Things were far from being ok, and he wasn't sure how much longer he could put up with it.

His heart was not only crushed but was being pulled in two different directions; being in love with two people at once was not easy for him. It was something he once believed was impossible to do, but now felt he couldn't live without either of them.

The pastor of Real Love Baptist Church was at a crossroad. He didn't know what to do—the pain inside his heart was too much to bear. He knew he couldn't continue to suffer the way he was, or hurt either of the two women he cared so deeply for, he wondered if he should just kill himself?

He sat alone crying his heart out at his desk inside the church's office. The palms of his hands were sweating profusely as he gripped the handle of a large caliber pistol. His hand shook uncontrollably as he held the gun firmly to the side of his head. Beads of sweat lined his forehead as his heart pounded like a beat of a drum—he didn't have the guts to pull the trigger, yet, he continued to grow more and more upset with himself. *Fuck!* He pressed the muzzle hard against his temple. Subsequently, he took the heavy weapon away from his head and laid it on top of his hardwood desk. He didn't know the first thing about psychiatry, but he knew there had to be a better way to solve his problem.

CHAPTER 14

"Mom, you know I don't like this dude," Chris said with his brows raised, as if his mom needed his permission before dating someone. "I don't get it; why do you keep going out with him; what could you possibly see in him?"

Valarie was offended by the tone of her son's voice. She was tempted to slap him hard across the face, but she held herself together as she responded. "Chris, Larry is a decent man. A respectful man—I like how he treats me and makes me feel, I really don't understand why you don't like him."

"I don't like how he acts," responded Chris. "I know I've only met him a few times, but his first few impressions weren't good ones. To me, he doesn't carry himself well, plus he looks real sneaky like he's up to something."

"Damn, is he dating me or you?" his mom asked.

"I don't like him, I just don't!"

"Well, suit yourself," his mom told him.

"I will," he said. "When you brought him to the restaurant the other night, he acted like he wanted to steal something."

"What is there to steal, Chris?" his mom snapped. "Some fucking silverware or some salt and pepper shakers? Tablecloths, placemats, what? What the fuck could he steal from your restaurant, Chris?"

It was clear to the young man that his mom was hurt and upset, so he eased up a bit to lessen the tension. "Mom, I'm sorry," he said in a whisper. "I didn't realize you liked him so much. I guess I'm just trying to look out for you, but I obviously went about it the wrong way," he said sincerely.

"Why is it that you and your father don't want me to be happy with anybody?" Valarie said with sadness in her voice. "I put up with his crap for years. I deserve to be happy with someone who treats me well."

"Mom, you can't compare me to dad," Chris said as he leaned in and wrapped his arms around her. "I've always wanted to see you happy. I can't speak for dad, but he doesn't have anything to do with this."

"He has everything to do with it, Chris," his mom said. "You've always sided with him, and you've been upset with me ever since I left him."

"That's not true."

"Yes, it is," his mom said. "You've always wanted your father and me to get back together, no matter how many times I've tried to tell you he's not right for me, you refused to accept it. Larry treats me the way I've always wanted to be treated."

Chris listened intently to what his mom was saying. He knew she was a strong but very sensitive woman who had endured more than her share of turmoil and stress after being left to raise him the best way she could. His dad had abandoned them when he was just a year old, so he realized she'd made a valid point. His dad would oftentimes show up unannounced, pretending as though he was a loving father who was trying to spend time with his son, but spending alone time with Valarie seemed to be the only thing on his agenda. He acted as though they were still a couple, and whenever she refused to have sex with him—things often turned violent—he then took what he wanted, feeling as though she had no right to say no. Valarie could never bring herself to file charges against him—she found it easier to endure whatever he dished at her.

Chris pulled his mom closer to him and kissed her on the cheek. He genuinely wanted to see her happy—he knew she deserved it more than anyone. He wanted her to experience what it felt like to be in a loving relationship, and if she felt Larry Kokane was the man for her, as her son, he knew she would need his full support. "So where do you and Larry plan on going tonight?" he said in a caring voice.

"To the Smith Center," his mom said, wondering why his attitude had shifted all of a sudden? "We both happen to be big fans of classical music, so we thought we'd go there to relax a bit."

"Well, if you find yourself hungry after listening to your weird music, I can always have your favorite dish waiting for you," he teased.

"Seafood gumbo, or baby back ribs?"

"Whichever you prefer."

"Probably the ribs."

"Done," he said.

"Thank you, son, I love you."

"I love you too, mom," he said with a smile. "I hope you and Larry enjoy yourselves tonight. I just want you to bring him by the restaurant again, you know Chris's Place always aim to please."

Valarie couldn't help but smile at her son. She realized he was giving Larry a second chance, and she appreciated him for doing so. She also knew he'd be more receptive; something she knew her man would appreciate. "We'll be there, and we'll be so delighted if you'd come out to serve us yourself."

"It would be my pleasure," he said with a grin. "I'll be your personal chef and waiter, so make sure y'all leave me a fat tip," he said as he burst out laughing. Chris knew that in order to keep his mom happy, he had to support her one hundred percent.

All eyes were fixated on Danielle and Erica as they strode through the carnival. Erica wore her black form-fitting lowrider jeans, some red six-inch stilettos, and a red midriff shirt that exposed her tiny waistline.

Danielle's outfit was phenomenal. She wore a pair of strapless heels that showed off her perfect feet, and a white spandex bodysuit that could stop traffic. Her skimpy attire left no room for the imagination, and absolutely no room for error—the wrong move would have definitely spelled disaster for her.

The rear of Danielle's bodysuit was devoured by her ample mouthwatering backside as it sank deeply into its crevasse—the cheeks wiggled like jello with each step she took, causing onlookers to wonder whether or not she was wearing panties? The fatness of her crotch was eye-catching. Her labia resembled two packs of cigarettes tied together, making the gap between her legs look like an invitation.

Danielle's large breasts pressed tightly against the fabric of her blouse's thin material, making her nipples protrude as if she weren't wearing a bra, sudden movement of any kind would have certainly caused spillage.

"Goddam, look at these hoes," a man said to his friend as they crossed paths.

Danielle glanced at Erica, then returned her attention back to the two men, she couldn't believe how disrespectful one of them were. "That describes your mama, not us."

"Don't let that shit get to you, girl," Erica said. "He's just mad 'cause we look better than the bitch he got at home."

"I wish she was with him so I could take her from him," Danielle said, purposely making her ass clap as she shook her hips.

"He like what he saw that's why he said that—probably hurt him to look at something he knows he can never have?"

"His friend was kind of cute though. You should have got at that."

"For what, if he was any kind of man, his ass would've stopped and got at me," Erica said, sounding full of herself. "My daddy ain't having that anyway."

"Your daddy, who is your daddy?" Danielle said, surprised. "I didn't know you had a daddy; you've never said anything to me about him."

Erica proceeded to put on a fake smile, regretting the fact that, once again, she'd misspoke.

"Who is he, ma?"

"You don't know him," said Erica.

"When are you gonna let me meet him then?"

"He lives in California. It might be a while before he comes back to Vegas."

"Not if his baby is out here," Danielle said. "It shouldn't. Why are you calling him your daddy if he's not going out of his way to come see you?"

"Girl, let's leave this conversation alone. I'll let you meet him when the time is right. I hate that I even brought it up."

"Okay, if you say so," Danielle said, noticing the sudden change in Erica's demeanor. With so much drama going on at the church, she wondered if Pastor Armstrong was the man she was referring to as daddy? Better yet, could her young friend be the woman he was caught cheating with, she wondered? Danielle definitely had her own suspicions but knew better than to keep pestering the teen with questions; she didn't want to make her feel any more uncomfortable than she already was.

"You know my birthday is coming up soon, right?" Erica said suddenly.

"How can I forget when you keep telling me it's on the 25th?"

121

"You know it," Erica said with a smile. "You know what I want from you for my birthday?"

"I guess I'll know when you tell me," Danielle said sarcastically, still wondering who the mystery man was that the teen had mentioned.

Erica looked at Danielle's body with admiration, pursing her lips before answering. "I want a bodysuit just like the one you're wearing. Same color and everything. That thang looks banging on you, girl."

Danielle smiled as she looked at Erica, she was more than impressed to see that she had such good taste.

"I like it a lot," Erica said as she continued to stare.

"It's not the suit, baby, it's the body that's in it," Danielle said as she struck a pose.

"That too," the teen agreed. "You're fine as hell without a doubt, but my eyes are on the outfit. Am I good for one or what?"

"Don't trip, ma, you got that," Danielle told her. "Don't expect to look the way I look in it though."

"Are you coming to my party?"

"Shit, where else am I gon' be—my black ass is in there," she said with a chuckle. "Where you gon' have it?"

"My apartment," said Erica. "It ain't gon' be nothing major. I'm only inviting a handful of people, so it's not like I'll need a lot of space. Just make sure you're there and you'll see how I'll look in my outfit."

"I told you, I'm there," Danielle said. She wondered if the man Erica referred to as daddy would be there as well—she wouldn't dare bring up the subject again—she'd just sit back and wait to find out.

"Let's get out of here," suggested the teen. "I cannot keep walking around in these damn shoes. My pinky toe is hurting like a muthafucka."

"Come on, ma, let's go," Danielle said.

As they made their way toward the carnival's exit, they continued to attract a lot of attention, mostly everyone seemed to be in awe, some even seemed to wonder what their prices were?

CHAPTER 15

L ife for Pastor Armstrong could no longer be described as peaches and cream. Every morning when he opened his eyes, instead of it feeling like home-sweet-home, it seemed to him like he'd woke up in prison—a nightmare would probably be a better way to describe it.

It's very unfortunate when an inmate dreams he's in a different place, but when he opens his eyes the next morning, he's suddenly brought back to a reality that he thought was over, leaving him to wonder why God would play such an evil trick?

It's a way of life that most people probably wouldn't be able to fathom, but for those in prison, they know that it's something that comes with the territory, unlike the distraught pastor who knew nothing about the other side of the fence, although he'd heard many inmates speak of it when he preached at jails. Now he had first-hand experience what the inmates meant when they said they saw no reason to get out of bed some mornings, because they knew the same things awaited them on a daily basis; the same environment; the same people; the same suffering; the same drawn-out torture; the same dead-end routine, day after day. No one in their right mind would want to climb out of bed just to endure something so inhumane, whether they're trapped inside of a literal prison, or one they created in their own mind, and Pastor Buddy Armstrong was no exception.

He woke up every morning feeling like he was in a foreign country. Nothing inside his home was familiar to him anymore, and his wife treated him as though he was a total stranger. Not just any stranger, but one from a third-world country, as if they'd come from two different cultures where language barriers divided them completely, making it nearly impossible for them to communicate.

It was 4:05 AM; his eyes had been open since 3:15.

He stared into complete darkness as he laid in a bed that was uncomfortable; a bed that was supposed to only be intended for guests who had come from out of town to visit, never once did he think it would be slept in by him.

The only light inside the room came from the streetlights that lined Madison Street, and they seemed to illuminate the empty space beside him. It was a blatant reminder that his wife was absent in bed next to him, sending a shockwave of sadness even deeper into his conscience, triggering a dagger-like pain that consumed his heart.

This had become an everyday feeling for him. Misery and darkness had infiltrated his soul; his eyes were filled with water as he thought of what once was—he was very aware of how much he missed his wife.

Although she was only a few feet away in the next bedroom, their non-salvageable bond made it feel like they were worlds apart. Pastor Armstrong loved his wife immensely, but her lack of reciprocation made it clear to him how much she felt the exact opposite.

Tears dripped from his eyelashes as he lay on his side. Something he found himself doing often…crying his eyes out until he fell back to sleep.

Hours passed before he woke up again. He thought he'd died and went to heaven when he opened his eyes to sunshine, and the sweet melody of his wife's voice.

"Buddy, I'm going to meet with my attorney this afternoon. Do you have any special requests before our divorce goes through?" she said from his bedroom doorway—fully dressed with her purse dangling loosely from her shoulder.

"Willa, can we work this out?" he said sadly, seeking compassion by batting his eyes.

"We are working it out," she said, unsympathetically. "We're working it out by ending it."

"C'mon, baby, let's talk about this. You know I love you, Willa," he said as he sat up.

"You keep your love 'cause I don't want it," she said unremorsefully, pulling the door shut.

The small glimmer of hope he had left was shattered in only a few seconds. He couldn't believe how quickly his life had soured. For a moment he thought it might turn out to be a good day when he heard her voice, but as soon as she pulled the door shut, it immediately felt like a good day to die!

CHAPTER 16

"**M**an, I see they got the club all taped off across the street," said Larry Kokane as he snatched the office door open to get a better look. He and the maintenance man Nino had just arrived to work, they often talked in the morning before starting their shifts. Although they both lived in the apartment complex, they rarely saw each other outside the job—they seemingly preferred to do their mingling while on the clock.

"Yeah, they had another senseless killing over there last night," said Nino as he sat in a chair, eating a banana. "All I did was nod when I saw it on the news this morning. It's always black on black too, you don't ever see white folks killing each other the way we do."

"Ain't that the truth," Larry said as he spun around, holding the knob on the door as it shut lightly behind him. "Probably had something to do with a woman too."

"It always does," Nino told him. "I know twat is good but it ain't that damn good."

"I guess it all depends on the woman," Larry said as his smile grew. "My girl Valarie got that snapper for real," he said with emphasis. "I don't know what it is about it, but it's addicting."

"Is it worth killing somebody over, better yet, is it worth dying for?" asked Nino.

"It all depends," said Larry. "I can't just say yes or no without giving it some thought. I'm telling you, man, my baby got that bomb."

"Ahh, you're just whipped. She done put that thang on your ass," said Nino.

"Shiiit, whipped ain't the word," Larry said, laughing. "I'm whipped, beat, stomped, kicked, dragged, smashed and everything else."

"At least you're being honest."

"Man, this woman done put something on me that I can't explain."

"She dropped that bomb on you, huh?" Nino said, grinning. "Bomb twat, bomb head, bomb asshole, bomb everything!"

"She got all that," the apartment manager admitted. "It don't matter what I'm doing, man, I just can't get my mind off her. It's like I eat, sleep and breathe her. I've been meaning to look up pussy and asshole on the internet to find out how many calories it got, 'cause that's all I've been eating lately."

"Sounds scary but fun," Nino said as he rubbed his hands together. "Are you in love with her, or are you just hooked on how she pleases you?"

"Man, it's gotta be the pussy," said Larry Kokane, denying the fact that he might be in love.

"I don't think I want no sex that good," said Nino. "If I gotta think about whether or not it's worth dying or killing over, I wouldn't be fuckin' with no woman with something that dangerous between her legs. You might want to consider leaving her alone, 'Kane."

Larry turned and looked at his employee, as if he couldn't believe what had just come from his mouth, if looks could kill, Nino would have died on the spot. "Leave her alone for what, so you can mess with her."

"You got that right!" Nino said as he burst out laughing.

Larry nodded and giggled before replying, "You're something else, Nino. I'll tell her you wanna know if she got any sisters."

"Sisters, cousins, aunts, mama—whoever," Nino said as he continued laughing. "Good twat might run in the family. She can hook me up with any one of her family members."

"You don't give a damn who it is, you just don't wanna be left out?"

"You got that right," Nino said again.

"Man, I feel you," replied the office manager.

"It's been a minute since I've had something like what you're talkin' about. Good all-around women are hard to find these days."

"You ain't never lying," Larry said as he walked back towards the office door and peeked through the blinds. It was something he did out of habit, thinking he might miss out on something, and if he hadn't looked when he did, he wouldn't have seen Erica's car leaving the parking lot. "The young girl in 7 acts like she can't stay still. Her young ass is always on the move."

"Probably goin' to pick up a lil' somethin'-somethin'," said Nino, "I be smelling weed every time I go past there. It don't be none of that regulated dispensary shit either, it be that strong street shit."

"Yeah, I've smelled it a few times myself," said Larry. "We can't knock it though 'cause we've all been there—a little maryjane every now and then ain't never hurt nobody."

"Amen to that," said Nino.

"That's probably what the preacher man be in there sayin'. I think he spends more time with her than he do his wife?"

"For each his own," said Nino. "I try my best to stay out of other grown folks' business, 'cause I damn sure don't want nobody in mine."

Larry was offended by his employee's remark but decided to keep his feelings to himself. He considered sharing with Nino that he'd called the pastor's wife to inform her of her husband's infidelity, but he knew the man would probably turn his nose up at him. Snitching was a very common practice in the black community but was only okay if it remained a secret. It was a very unpopular activity if word got out, and there were consequences to suffer for those who were caught. *Oh well, I guess everybody who's skin to me ain't kin to me?* Larry recognized that just because someone is black doesn't mean they're his people. He knew that he had to keep his secret to himself—it was the best and only way to assure his safety.

"Man, have you seen the one girl that visits sometimes?"

"The one that drives the red truck?"

"Lord have mercy!" Nino said with emphasis.

"Now that's a bad bitch," responded Larry. "I can't have no bitch that goddam fine. You gon' have to kill somebody over that fa'sho."

"She is a bad motherfucker," said Nino. "It brightens my day every time I see her. I can't do nothin' but smile when I look at her."

"Sounds like stalking, but in this case, I understand," Larry said before laughing. It was ten minutes before nine when he glanced at his watch, the time that he usually began his shift. "Well, maybe with the club being shut down, it'll be a lot less traffic around here."

"I'm sure it will," Nino said as he climbed to his feet. "Let me go ahead and get this day started. I gotta get over there to fix Ms. Marilyn's air conditioner. She's been hounding me about it for 2 or 3 days."

Ms. Marilyn was a longtime tenant of the J and J apartments. She relied on a cane to walk due to a bad knee, but she was highly respected by everyone in the area. She was not one who complained often, but when she found a problem worth complaining about, she didn't stop fussing until it was resolved.

"I'm so tired of that woman leaving voicemails. Every message on the machine came from her," Larry said with frustration in his voice.

"Yeah, I'ma get over there now before she calls the cops on me," Nino said, joking as he inched closer to the door.

"That woman ain't gon' call the cops on nobody. Her crazy ass might pull a gun or knife on you, but you ain't gotta worry about her calling the police," Larry said while adjusting his belt.

"If she threatens me in any kind of way, 'Kane, she might as well turn around and put cuffs on herself, 'cause I'm gon' definitely call the police on her," Nino joked as he headed out the door.

As soon as the office door shut, Larry reached for the phone to check on Valarie.

CHAPTER 17

The congregation at Real Love Baptist Church was in a downslide. It was obvious to Pastor Armstrong as he stood at the pulpit overlooking the pew, that less and less members showed up each week.

He was of the opinion that the only thing that caused his congregation to shrivel was that they missed the presence of his wife Willa.

The pastor knew how significant his wife was to the church, especially to its large female population, so as he stood behind the pulpit delivering his message, he decided to speak directly to their psyche by apologizing to her in absentia, admitting his shortcomings, in a desperate attempt to stop his remaining congregation from shrinking further.

He stood like a tyrant at the pulpit overlooking the audience, sweating profusely and appearing to look remorseful—trying his best to win back as many hearts as possible. "I'll start by reminding everyone that the Bible says we should forgive others as we would want our father in heaven to forgive us," he said, trying to sound convincing. He then pulled a handkerchief from his jacket pocket and wiped the sweat from his forehead before continuing. "The Bible tells us that we should not hold grudges, nor let our hearts become hard. I know I messed up by stepping out on my wife, but I'm only human just like the rest of you," he said before pausing. "God knows that I'm terribly sorry for breaking my wife's heart, and for embarrassing the church. I'll be the first to admit how wrong I was, but I hope you'll all find it in your hearts to someday forgive me."

The pastor was fully aware that several members of the church were in touch with his heartbroken wife. He was hoping someone would call her on his behalf and convince her to give him a second chance.

The congregation appeared to be lending him their full attention, so he continued to beg for mercy like his life depended on it. "Not forgiving someone is equivalent to drinking poison and expecting the other person to die," he said as he paced the floor, giving what he'd said time to sink in. "We all know it doesn't work like that; we're only harming ourselves when we choose not to forgive."

"Amen to that!" yelled one of the deacons.

Pastor Armstrong made eye contact with some of the members of his pew, and delivered a plea filled with desperation. "I love this church and its members more than life itself—I beg all of you to please forgive me. Dig as deep as you need to and take as much time as you need, but I need another chance to redeem myself," he said before laying the microphone down and leaving the pulpit.

Several members wiped tears from their eyes as he walked away, several more could be heard sniveling and sobbing.

UNGODLY

The pastor was joined by Erica as soon as he set foot inside his office. She'd observed everything as she stood in the shadows, still, no one had a clue that she was his mistress.

"What the hell was that?" she said with her hand on her hip, staring directly at him, awaiting a reply.

"I'm trying to do what I can to save the church."

"Sounds to me like you're trying to save your marriage," she said with anger in her voice.

Pastor Armstrong just stared at her. He thought her jealous attitude was kind of cute but seemed to feel that her timing was a bit off. He admired how much his young lover appreciated him, but he wasn't in the mood for any arguing. They did everything together, read the Bible, took walks in the park, talked about everything under the sun—and had a very exciting sex life regardless of their age difference—he really enjoyed the time he spent with her, but for some reason, she wasn't enough. He needed Willa; he couldn't live without her. She was his heart, his soulmate, his lifelong companion— Willa Armstrong was his everything. That's one thing he knew for sure, he just wished he knew what to do to get her back. The fact that he didn't was killing him.

He went home every night just to appease her. And, although they weren't on speaking terms, they seemed to always know whether or not the other was home, so he made it appear as though he'd learned from his mistake and was being faithful.

From counseling so many members of his congregation, he was aware that there was ample time to file the necessary paperwork to halt their divorce proceedings, and he was holding out hope that she would perhaps file them? He figured everything rested with his latest sermon.

He figured if what he preached would encourage enough people in the congregation to give his wife a call, he truly believed he'd have a decent chance.

"So, is that what you're trying to do?" Erica asked with her arms crossed.

"What?" the pastor said, pretending to be dumb.

"You know damn well what I'm talking about," the teen retorted. "Are you attempting to save your marriage?"

"Young lady, for the second time, I'm trying to save my church—my wife is perhaps the only one who can help me do it. You can't tell me you don't see how much they miss her."

"I haven't heard not one person in this church say shit. I think you're the one who misses her?"

Pastor Armstrong didn't respond, the entire ordeal began to upset him.

"I guess you're saying if you can keep her, you can save your church?" she said before pausing. "So where does that leave me if you and her get back together?"

Pastor Armstrong began nodding his head. The last thing he wanted to do was hurt her feelings, so he spoke to her with as much compassion as he could muster. "Sweetheart, I don't have time to think about any of that right now. This church is my life, Erica. It means more to me than anything else in the world. The future of it is the only thing that matters to me right now."

"So, I don't mean nothin' to you?"

"You know that's not what I'm saying, Erica," he said sincerely. "What I'm saying is if my wife comes back, all the members who left will come back with her. That's really important to me, Erica. Life will no longer have meaning if I lose my church."

Erica watched as tears welled in his eyes then rolled down his cheeks, she wondered if they were really for the church, or for his wife—she assumed the latter, and spun off.

His heart sank as he watched her leave. He even considered chasing after his young lover, but a church full of people prevented him from doing so.

He sat erectly at his desk, dumbfounded—eyes zeroed in on the bottom drawer, the one that held his pistol, so he reached for the handle and pulled it open.

He stared at the shiny black hardware that lay comfortably inside the drawer and considered eating one of its hollow-point bullets. He just wanted all of his suffering to end, but quickly decided it wasn't the time nor place.

He wanted life as he knew it to return back to normal, but Willa Armstrong would determine that. Whether she knew it or not, he felt she was the one who held all the keys.

CHAPTER 18

For the first time in his life, Larry Kokane was completely content with having just one woman, it was the one thing he couldn't fathom before meeting Valarie. Never once had he had a woman who shared her all with him, making him feel so good reciprocating.

He appreciated the fact that she took great pride in satisfying him completely. She was always thorough and patient when it came to fulfilling his needs and multiple fantasies and seemed to get much joy out of doing so, and to keep things fair, he did the same for her.

He thought about her from the moment he opened his eyes in the morning until he went to bed at night, he knew he had undeniably fallen in love with her, and there wasn't a damn thing he could do about it.

He enjoyed each minute he spent with her. They both had an insatiable appetite for sex, so, naturally, it became their favorite pastime.

"Oooh, baby, give it to me," she said as she rode him backwards in the middle of the office floor of the J and J apartments. "Ooooooh, it feels so good, baby!"

The office manager watched as her wet vagina slid back and forth, glistening the length of his member, he couldn't get enough of her slippery hole.

Valarie was fully aware that her man would be working late that evening, so she stopped by to chat while he did some last-minute paperwork—she had no idea they would end up sprawled across the floor. "Put your finger in my ass, baby," she said boldly, trying to bring out all the freak he had in him. She then closed her eyes while squeezing her sensitive nipples before reaching between her legs to stimulate her clit with her finger. "I need you to fuck my asshole with your finger, baby," she said again, clearly wanting to be double-penetrated as she continued to ride him.

Larry Kokane was not one to pass up a great opportunity. He placed his middle finger inside his mouth to salivate it, then spread her ass cheeks and slid his finger inside.

"Yesss, baby. Yes!" she screamed loudly. "Oh my god, I'm coming! Come with me, baby. Come with me!" she said with her eyes shut as her entire body began to stiffen.

Larry laid his head on the floor and let his arms fall to his sides after releasing his sperm inside of her. He was spent while lying breathlessly on the office floor—he loved how Valarie made love to him. She seemed to want some of his lovin' every time he saw her, and he was more than eager to accommodate her.

He noticed how she had kept her freaky side hidden the first few times they slept together, but the woman who once pretended to be shy and conservative, left nothing to the imagination when it came to sex. "You ain't no joke, girl," he said, panting. "I think I might end up marrying you one day."

Valarie sensed the sincerity in his voice, but he continued talking before she could respond.

"I've never had nobody freak me the way you do. I never knew lovemaking could be so fun."

"I'm glad you enjoy me, darling," she said, smiling. "I'm not saying you're not serious, but I need you to do me a huge favor."

"I'm listening," he told her.

Valarie looked her man square in the eye and spoke candidly and passionately simultaneously. "When you speak to me about marriage, please talk about it because you mean it; don't speak on it because you like how I fuck you, okay?"

"I got you, sweetheart," he said as he pulled her toward him, kissing her lightly on the forehead.

From previous conversations, he knew marriage was something she took seriously, and regretted being so careless with his choice of words. "I wasn't playing," he said under his breath.

"Did you just say something, babe?"

"No, I'm just thinking out loud," he lied.

Office hours were over for the day, so Valarie leaned her head against his chest and carelessly draped her arm over his slender body. They held each other gently until they fell asleep.

In the subconscious mind of most African-Americans, because of a past that had its share of tragedies, it was rare to join collectively in the city of Las Vegas to celebrate any event without some form or expectation of being harassed or spied upon by law enforcement, who apparently had nothing better to do with their time.

Miraculously Erica's birthday party hadn't been crashed yet. She had finally reached the milestone of eighteen—an age where she was still tender but legal, and she wanted to embrace her womanhood by enjoying an evening filled with food, fun and something extra-curricular with a group of old and new friends alike as she embarked on a new stage in her life known as adulthood.

All of her closest friends were in attendance. The extravagant over-the-top Bubbles, the wannabe-tough-guy Menace, the one and only Dominique, of whom she suspected was gay, and her drop-dead gorgeous friend and co-worker Danielle. There were also a few other attendees that she didn't know too well, as well as friends of friends whom she didn't invite, but they weren't causing any trouble, so she allowed them to stay in an effort to help liven things up.

Erica was really excited about her special day. A day she especially wanted her mom to be part of, but, so far, Lisa Miles was nowhere to be found.

The over-developed teen entered the living room from her bedroom wearing the clad spandex bodysuit Danielle gave her as a gift. She immediately caught the attention of the partygoers who were already dancing and appeared to be enjoying themselves—the party was just getting into full swing, she hoped everything would remain peaceful.

"Oh my goodness!" the pastor said under his breath when he saw her standing inches from her bedroom doorway. He was straddling the arm of the love seat when she noticed him, he couldn't take his eyes off her body as she approached.

"Hey, daddy," she said before glancing down at his crotch. She then raised her hand to cover her mouth then leaned in towards him and whispered to him. "Good folks are hard to come by. Glad you came by."

"Happy birthday, beautiful," he said as he checked out her outfit. "I won't be staying long. I just wanted to stop by and wish you a happy birthday."

The teen was fully aware that the pastor was way out of his element. She knew he wasn't accustomed to being around young partygoers, he was only there because it was her birthday. "Come here I wanna show you something," she said while tugging his shoulder.

The reserved pastor quickly stood, following the teen to her bedroom. Danielle came out of nowhere and intervened.

"Where y'all goin'?" she said loudly, happy to see Erica flaunting the outfit she'd given her as a gift. It hugged every nook and cranny of her curvaceous body; she was surprised at how good it looked on her.

"My toilet is stopped up, he's about to fix it before it runs over. That's the last thing I need to happen on my birthday."

"Uh-uh, that wouldn't be good," Danielle frowned, stepping aside. She watched as Erica's buttocks shook like gelatin as she entered the bedroom—Pastor Armstrong couldn't seem to take his eyes off of it.

Uh, I'm scared of y'all Danielle said to herself before returning to the dance floor. She'd already downed two apple martinis, so not only was she feeling wonderful, but she was more than eager to strut her stuff. "Heyyy," she said as she started dancing, bumping hips with the girl that was closest to her. She then eyed the woman and thought she was pretty but slender, and too young for her taste, so she left the dance floor once the song ended—it wasn't because she was tired of dancing, but because she found herself having to pee.

She stood between the kitchen and living room praying Pastor Armstrong had already fixed the toilet, then made a beeline through Erica's bedroom trying to get to the toilet but heard strange noises upon reaching the bathroom door. *Damn* she thought to herself while pressing her ear to the door. *I hope they're not doing what I think they're doing?*

She placed her hand on the doorknob then turned it slowly as she peeked inside. *Oh my god!* She was shocked when she saw Erica sitting completely naked on the edge of the bathroom sink, legs wrapped tightly around the pastor's back as he drove his hips forward repeatedly—his brute force shook her entire body.

Danielle continued to stare in disbelief. She couldn't see the pastor's facial expressions, but she heard his grunting and moaning as he continued to pound his young lover's vagina like a world class boxer pummeling a speed bag, his pants and underwear bunched around his ankles.

Ain't this a bitch Danielle mumbled but refused to avert her eyes away from the action. She looked down and saw his exposed legs, but his long suit jacket prevented her from seeing his ass, he couldn't seem to get enough of his young mistress' jewel. The pastor's massive shoulders obscured Erica's view of the door, but judging from the noise the teen was making, it appeared that the birthday girl was having an awesome time. Danielle considered using her cell phone to capture the moment but decided against it. Instead, she pulled the bathroom door shut just as softly as she'd pushed it open and headed back to the living room to rejoin the party—using the bathroom suddenly became a blur to her.

Moments later, the couple engaged in the forbidden sex came from the bedroom, both wiping sweat from their forehead, pretending as though nothing had happened between them.

Danielle sipped a cold beer as she stood a few feet outside of the bedroom doorway, concealing the anger she felt boiling inside her. "Did he fix it?" she said the moment Erica walked up to her.

"Yeah, it's fixed," Erica said smiling, too young and dumb to realize Danielle was holding the plunger that had been left in the kitchen earlier that day to unstop the sink, she instead, reached for the beer Danielle clutched in her opposite hand.

I bet it is Danielle thought as she released her grip.

"You want this back?"

"Nah, keep it, ma."

"Thank you—it's so hot in here," the teen said as she raised the beer to her lips.

Without saying a word, Pastor Armstrong turned and headed for the front door, Erica was right on his heels when he pulled it open.

"Are you leaving?" she said after they stepped outside.

"Yeah, sweetie, it's time for me to go," he said as he looked around, then grabbed a handful of the teen's ass.

"Don't start nothin' you can't finish," she said jokingly.

Pastor Armstrong released his grip, then felt himself experiencing a recurring erection, he loved how she looked in her bodysuit. "I don't know why I can't get enough of you." He thought that his groping had gone unnoticed, but it was witnessed by the office manager as he peeked through the blinds of the main office—Larry Kokane wanted to strangle him.

This pedophile, cradle-rocking, bitch motherfucker thought the office manager while easing away from the window, in an effort to keep his temper in tact. He and Valarie had just woken up after falling asleep on the office floor, it wasn't exactly what he'd hoped to wake up to.

It wasn't the first time he'd seen the pastor touch the teen inappropriately, he considered calling the police or serving an eviction notice, he was totally against that kind of behavior, especially on the premises of the J and J apartments.

It crossed his mind to call Willa Armstrong to bring her husband's unrelenting diabolical behavior to her attention, but a sudden touch from Valarie gained his full attention. He got sidetracked as they made love again

145

on the hard office floor—the pastor and Erica were suddenly the farthest thing from his mind.

CHAPTER 19

"Don't hurt yourself," Valarie said with a giggle.

"What—did I do something?" Larry said, trying to sound innocent.

"I see you staring at all this ass, you know damn well what I'm talkin' about," his woman said before heading toward the snack stand.

They were over six months into their relationship, and she loved the fact that he never changed the way he looked at her. His admiration for her made her feel like a princess who'd found her knight and shining armor—she truly believed he would be her husband. She thought things were going much too well for him not to be.

The men she met in the past only seemed to want to have sex with her, but Larry Kokane proved his feelings were genuine. It became obvious to her that he didn't come around only when he wanted sex from her, or when it was beneficial for him, but he came around because he had a real interest in her. He was the only man she'd ever encountered who asked her questions about her childhood; what schools she attended; her dating history as well as her future plans. He showed great interest in getting to know her inside and out, he was always there for her whenever she needed him.

She loved how he made her feel on a daily basis—he pampered her, catering to her every need, and if he continued to do so, she had no doubt that he would be her husband.

Larry smiled as he watched her stride away wearing a tiny yellow two-piece bikini, swinging her ass hard on purpose, because she knew he was watching. *Look at that ass. Lord have mercy!*

They spent their afternoon bathing in the sun at Cowabunga Bay—the king of all Las Vegas' waterparks, where hundreds of men and women paraded around in their skimpy bikinis, showing off their chiseled, curvy physiques they'd worked so hard to get—there was plenty of eye candy for everyone.

For a woman in her late fifties, Valarie's body didn't have any stretch marks, cellulite, sagging skin, or anything that fell below the standard of what it meant to be perfect. In no way shape or form was she out of shape, she looked more like a woman in her early thirties, her entire exterior was impeccable.

Larry saw groups of men, women and children as he gazed around the park, some of whom were there to have fun as a family, while others only seemed to be interested in scoping out the eye candy.

Valarie returned momentarily, carrying two massive hot dogs topped with chili and cheese, and two soft drinks that nearly fell from her hands. She immediately began laughing when Larry stopped the items from falling.

"Thank you," she said softly. "I saw you still getting an eyeful when I walked off. You didn't hurt yourself, did you?"

"I'll answer that later," he said while inspecting his food. He had never once met a woman as caring as Valarie, he knew he couldn't have asked for a better woman. "I try to appreciate your beauty every chance I get, baby. Sometimes I still can't believe how beautiful you are—it's so exhilarating and rewarding to know you're mine."

"Thank you, sweetie," she said as she sat on his lap and kissed him softly on the forehead. She watched as he ate his chili-cheese dog in such a manner as if he'd never eaten before, but she didn't let it stop her from expressing herself. "I don't know why but it feels so good when I'm with you, Larry. I feel like I'm finally with the man that I'm meant to be with—as if it's where I should be for the rest of my life."

Larry Kokane did not respond after hearing the remark, but his heart was smiling uncontrollably. "I feel the same way, baby," he finally said. He'd wondered a few times what it would feel like to make Valarie his wife—he felt so relieved to hear she thought the same way he did—their kindred spirit had been confirmed, he thought. He knew they were too old to consider bearing children of their own, but if she was open enough to let him, he was more than willing to accept her adult son Chris as if he was his own, and love him unconditionally, as well as be the best stepdad a child could ever dream of having.

Larry glanced at his potential wife-to-be and wrapped his arm around her. The thought crossed his mind to propose to her, but he knew how important marriage was to her, so he bit his tongue to give it some more thought. He just wanted to be certain that he was ready to commit.

The once self-proclaimed player leaned forward and kissed Valarie on her exposed thigh, then bit the chili dog she held in her hand.

"Uh-uh, don't tease me like that," she said, frowning.

Larry looked at her with a burning desire that came from deep within, then placed his hand on her thigh as he licked his lips. "Teasing you how?"

"Don't kiss me there if you ain't gon' eat this pussy. You know that's my spot, and you know how crazy I get every time you do it," she said in a whisper.

"I'll do it for you if that's what you want, but if I do, we're going to jail," he said before laughing.

Valarie could do nothing but smile. She knew her man loved her just as much as she loved him—nothing or no one could have made her happier.

The evening after her eighteenth birthday party, Erica and Danielle found themselves surrounded by screaming children and excited women at one of Las Vegas' phenomena known as The Bend. It was a brand-new venue that hosted exquisite 4 Star restaurants, as well as a large shopping gallery that housed a medley of high-end brands.

The Bend was said to house the best of the best when it came to fashion—making the world-famous Forum Shops at Caesar's Palace a thing of the past.

"So, when were you going to tell me you're screwing the boss?" Danielle said bluntly as her leggings clung tightly to her shapely physique.

Erica's gut quickly formed a knot. She turned to Danielle with a look of bewilderment. "What are you talking about—I know you're just playing, right?"

"Don't play dumb, ma," Danielle told her. "I saw him digging you out last night on the bathroom sink, unless that's what you call fixing the toilet?"

Erica turned her nose up, then rolled her eyes—she couldn't believe that she was being confronted.

"If you still wanna lie and act like the pastor was in your bathroom doing some plumbing—keep it real and say he was in there laying pipe. How long have you been fuckin' him, Erica?"

The eighteen-year-old knew she was busted. She was more embarrassed than ever, but she knew she couldn't keep hiding the truth. "For a minute," she said in a low voice. "It started when I was living with them on Madison."

"So that's who you were referring to as daddy when we were at the carnival the other night?"

She hesitated a bit, then said, "Yeah."

"And it's also the reason Miss Willa hates you so much?"

"Danielle, you have to promise me that you won't say anything. Pastor Armstrong would have a fit if word got out."

"I won't mention it, ma—it ain't my business," Danielle said convincingly. "I was only asking you those questions a while back 'cause

Miss Willa suspected y'all was up to something. I thought she was crazy when she mentioned it to me."

"What did she say?"

"She didn't say too much of nothin' 'cause she didn't know nothin'," Danielle told her. "She asked if I knew somethin' about it and I told her no."

The teen paused and looked around, momentarily turning to face Danielle. "I'm pretty sure that I'm the reason they broke up," she began slowly. "She came and knocked on my door one night, and his ass was standing behind me, wearing only his boxers. She didn't see us doing nothin', but I'm sure she knew what was going on."

"She knocked on the door of your apartment?"

"Yeah."

"How does she know where you live at?"

"We don't know, that's the part we can't figure out, but it don't matter. It's too late to be worrying about any of that," said Erica.

"She never even mentioned that to me. I didn't even know she caught y'all together."

"I don't think she mentioned it to anybody," said Erica. "As far as I know, she just told the congregation she'd caught her husband with another woman, but I don't think she ever mentioned that it was me?"

"I commend her if that's how she did it. Do you know that for sure or are you just guessing?"

"You know how the church is," Erica said. "If they knew it was me, somebody would have definitely said something by now."

"She was suspicious of y'all when she brought it to my attention, but she hasn't mentioned it again since."

"Make sure you don't mention it either," Erica told her.

"Oh, I won't, I promise," Danielle said. "I still wouldn't believe it if I hadn't witnessed it with my own eyes—I don't know why somebody as young and fine as you is messing around with someone at least three times your age?"

"That's how life is sometimes," Erica said in a mature voice. "That's probably why they say we should always expect the unexpected."

"If you say so," Danielle said. "We can't change what's already happened, so we might as well just let sleeping dogs lie."

"I'm with you on that," said Erica.

"Well, ma, since we're out here, we may as well do some window shopping."

"We probably can't even afford to do that; they say all of this shit is high-end."

"Girl, stop playing," Danielle told her. "If you got that old bastard to buy you a car and put you in your own apartment, if you wanted to, I'm sure you can get him to buy you some of this shit."

"You're probably right," the teen agreed. "They say this stuff is really expensive though."

"So is that sweet young vagina," Danielle said. "Greatness costs what it cost, if he wants to keep getting it, he'll pay the price."

"Ooooh," Erica said before laughing. "You sound like you're my pimp or somethin'. I'm nobody's ho, so don't get it twisted."

"That's not what I'm sayin', ma," Danielle explained. "I'm just sayin' get it while you can. You're not going to be young and pretty forever, so do as they say and get it while the gettin' is good."

"Stop hating, Danielle," the teen said then struck a pose. "I'ma look like this until they put me in the ground, I don't know why you're holding your nuts on me."

"For one, I ain't got no nuts, and two, I'm just saying you better get everything you can before the next young bitch comes along," Danielle explained. "Get what you can while you got his attention."

"I will but I ain't trying to break him," Erica told her. She had genuine feelings for Pastor Armstrong—his money was not the only thing that piqued her interest.

"Are you in love with him?"

"I don't care about his money, Danielle. I appreciate everything he does for me, and it's not my intention to hurt him financially."

"I feel you, ma," Danielle said. "I'm not telling you to break him. I'm just sayin' if you decide you want somethin', don't be shy about askin' him to buy it."

"I know, but it's him that I care about, not his money. I personally think he's already done enough."

"It don't matter, let him do more that's what he's there for," Danielle told her. "It's not his first rodeo, he understands what his position is."

"I don't need nothin', I'm cool," said Erica.

Danielle looked at her friend and shook her head. She wasn't sure if the teen was just playing dumb, or if she was really that stupid? Whatever it was she was tired of trying to get through to her. "If you don't need nothin' that's cool, ma, but if you do decide that you want something, make his ass go into the church's building fund, the tithes, offering, or wherever! Make him do whatever he gotta do to make it happen—all I'm sayin' is, don't give him no breaks. Don't act like your young fine ass don't got it like that."

"I am fine, ain't I?" the teen laughed, then spun around to give her a clear view. "Let me know you recognize it then, but don't hate," she said with a grin.

Now why would I hate on you when I could have been had his old ass if I wanted him? Danielle thought. *Bitch, you lied about this shit when we first talked about it—I should go ahead and go against the grain and snatch his old ass up?...Nah, I'm cool.*

"Let's look around and see if we can find something cute. You know the most expensive shit be the ugliest," Erica said to change the subject.

The women took a tour of The Bend's property, but unfortunately couldn't find anything they could afford, however, they planned to return on a later date.

CHAPTER 20

It is highly impossible to predict the forces of nature. Some people's lives are like peaches and cream, and for reasons only known to the mother of nature, others' lives seem to careen out of control. It can be compared to driving down a slippery road. There's no reason to panic as long as you have control of the vehicle you're driving—but when your emotions become the driving force in your life—the moment you begin to lose control, there's no way to regain it until you crash, but, by then, it's too late.

Crashing seemed to be inevitable for Pastor Armstrong. His life had quickly become a slippery slope; swerving and fishtailing all over the place, hoping and praying that he wouldn't be unstable for long but he knew even that was not in his control.

He sat uncomfortably in his office a few hours before services one Sunday morning, hoping to put finishing touches on the day's sermon, but there were more people there than he anticipated.

It wasn't the first time some of his employees had shown up early for work, but they usually hung out in the lounge drinking coffee, eating breakfast, and shooting the breeze until some of the members started arriving for Sunday school.

For the most part, his office was usually his sanctuary, especially in the mornings when everyone knew he used the time to work on his sermons, but not everyone cared that he didn't want to be bothered.

"What was Ne-Ne doing in here?" Erica asked rudely after bursting into his office without knocking.

Pastor Armstrong glanced at her; he was not in the mood to deal with her attitude.

"I said what was she doing here?" she repeated when he didn't answer immediately.

Pastor Armstrong seemed extremely nervous, as if he'd just been caught with his pants down. "Not this morning, young lady," he said with trembling in his voice. "You see I'm trying to get my sermon together."

"Why was that bitch in here?" the teen said, making it clear that she didn't care about anyone else's feelings beside her own. "I have no problem with going to ask her if I need to."

"Erica, you don't question me about what I talk to my employees about," he said with anger in his voice. "Ne-Ne just wanted to ask me something."

"This early in the morning?"

"It doesn't matter what time it is, that ain't got nothin' to do with nothin'."

"I don't believe you," she said bluntly. "I don't believe she was asking you shit, and I know damn well she wasn't in here fixing shit. I think you and that funny looking bitch got something going."

"Erica, please!" Pastor Armstrong said with angst. "It's too early in the morning for this nonsense. I told you she just wanted to ask me something."

"Are you sure that's all?" she said, seeming to calm down.

He looked at her, frowned, and then rolled his eyes.

"Was that it for real, 'cause she was shaking those funny shaped hips pretty hard when I saw her leaving? I hope she wasn't in here flirting with you."

"She just asked me a question," the pastor said solemnly. "Don't go making a big deal out of nothing. Now if you don't mind, I'd like to get back to my sermon," he said as he looked at his watch.

"Alright," Erica said before heading toward the door. "I remember you used to tell your wife the same thing about us, and we both knew you were lying through your big teeth," she said before leaving.

Whew! he thought as he leaned back in his chair, massaging his temple trying to ease his mind. All he wanted was to feel like himself again, a sense of normalcy was all he hoped to accomplish.

Before he left home that morning, he was tempted to peek inside his wife's bedroom to make sure she was okay. At one point her well-being was his first priority. They were somewhat back on speaking terms, only speaking when it was necessary, but he was tempted to tell her that he hoped to see her at church since rumors had it that she planned to return?

Supposedly she expressed it to someone in the congregation, and it spread through the church like wildfire, the pastor thought it was great if the rumor was true, but since he was unsure about its accuracy, he didn't want it to seem like he was rushing her to forgive him, so he changed his mind about bothering her about it. He didn't want to ruin his chances of saving the church—he concluded that exercising patience was his only option.

He exhaled after taking a deep breath. His mind drew a blank as he stared at his notes—he had no idea how he'd become so selfish and reckless. If Erica had come to his office only minutes sooner, all hell would have broke loose if she had witnessed what him and Ne-Ne were up to.

The questionable devout pastor of Real Love Baptist Church finally picked up his pen to conclude his sermon. His heart began beating rapidly again as he thought of how close he'd come to being caught. Close calls had become more and more frequent over the past few months, he couldn't help but wonder how much longer it might be before he'd play it too close? His intuition warned him that it was only a matter of time. Pastor Armstrong was learning something new about himself, even though no sane person wanted to crash and burn, it was something about the danger of being caught that he found exciting—what he thought was a case of nervousness was a rush of adrenaline, and he knew he hadn't yet gotten his fill.

Pastor Armstrong knew in his own heart of hearts that he needed intervention from God, but still, instead of continuing his life and conducting himself like the respected pastor he was, he continued to live like a crash dummy—it was highly unlikely he'd keep getting away unscathed.

CHAPTER 21

Larry Kokane had always dreaded going shopping with a woman. It was something he had sworn off five years prior after a multitude of bad experiences, but if the expression *there's an exception to every rule* is true, then the magnificent Valarie Hill was his exception. She promised him that shopping with a woman could be fun for a man if it's done right, and he found himself enjoying every minute of it.

His eyes lit up time and time again as she tried on different types of lingerie, modeling sexily in front of him, eagerly seeking his opinion on everything she wore. He looked on as she paraded around like an experienced underwear model, trying her best to get a rise out of him—something he didn't hesitate to succumb to. She purchased everything he found to be attractive on her, not worrying about the cost, and left everything behind that didn't hold his attention.

The lengths a woman will go to please a man she thought to herself as they stood abreast at the counter.

The store clerk handed the credit card back to Valarie as Larry wrapped his arm around her. "It would be absolutely amazing if you could put all of this on at the same time."

Valarie smiled as she shifted her body closer to his. "It would take me too long to get naked if I did that," she said. "The goal is to wear as little as possible so you can get to my goods as quickly as possible, so wearing it all at once would defeat the purpose."

"I know that's right," he said while squeezing her shoulder. "It'll give me something new to look forward to for at least a week."

"Exactly," she said.

They held each other's hand tightly as they strolled out of the lingerie store, they seemed to fall deeper and deeper in love with each other.

"I have an amazing woman," he said as he kissed her softly on the forehead. "It feels more and more phenomenal every time I'm with you."

"And, I have a wonderful man," she said sincerely. "You have no idea how much you make my heart smile."

All he did was smile after hearing her comment. The old school player had never met a woman who made him feel so complete. He became more and more convinced they'd spend the rest of their lives together. He felt that all of the pieces of the puzzle had fallen into place, and he hoped he wasn't wrong by thinking that spending the rest of their lives together was inevitable? He and Valarie strode hand in hand through the mall's parking lot, joking and laughing about someday turning into senior citizens together, and in their heart of hearts, they knew it was only a matter of time before it would turn into reality…

"Damn, who is this?" whispered the man when he exited the mini-mart and saw the shapely woman struggling with her gas cap. He noticed that no one was accompanying her so he approached her with caution to see if she needed some help. "What's the problem, miss, you seem to be having some trouble?" he said, displaying a set of perfect white teeth. "Can I help you with that?"

"Absolutely," she said as she stepped aside. "Stupid me managed to get my key stuck; it's embarrassing."

"It's not just you it happens to all of us," he said. With ease, the tall, muscular gentleman removed the gas cap, then pulled the keys out, handing them to her.

All she did was stare before responding. "Thank you. You're such a gentleman, a handsome one at that," she said as she reached for her keys, purposely closing her hand around his.

"My pleasure, ma'am. I'm glad I could help," he said before pausing. "By the way I'm Tyree—it's a pleasure to meet you."

"It's a pleasure to meet you too, Tyree. I'm Willa," she said, blushing.

"Nice to meet you, Willa."

"Nice to meet you, too," she said while standing awkwardly. She found it hard to act normal in front of a man that wasn't her husband—she hadn't had any new interests in nearly four decades. "Are you married?" she managed to say.

"Not yet," he said calmly. "Not that it's something to be proud of, but I'm as single as one can be. I guess I'm just waiting for the right one. How 'bout yourself?"

"This isn't anything to be proud of either, but I'm currently going through a divorce," she said with reluctance in her voice.

"Well, welcome to the nothing-to-be-proud-of club," he said humorously.

She laughed and found it refreshing. "Thank you. Not a nasty one, but a divorce nonetheless."

"Well, it's always best to end it amicably," Tyree said as he stared at her.

"Are you speaking from experience?"

"No, just in general," he told her. "I've been through many things in my forty-seven years of life, but fortunately for me, divorce is not one of them, at least not yet," he said, smiling.

"Good for you," she said, admiring his good looks. "It's not something I regret; I just think it's time I do something different."

"I feel so sorry for him—he sure is losing something beautiful," he said while nodding his head. "Whose idea was it to part ways?"

"Mine," she said quickly. "I think maybe I got too old for him, because I caught him with a much younger woman."

"Shame on him," Tyree said smoothly. "Personally, from looking at you I think you're perfect—older women have always been my cup of tea."

The older woman found herself excited about meeting a younger man, especially one who seemed to be interested in her, an uncontrollable smile suddenly appeared on her face. The way Tyree pronounced his words was a big turn-on for her, so she kept talking to him so he could keep replying. "I could definitely use a friend," she said in a voice that was sexier than her natural one. "It would be great having someone to talk to from time to time."

"I'd love to be your friend, Willa, it's been such a pleasure speaking with you."

"If you enjoy it so much, why are you leaving?"

Tyree looked confused. "I'm not. Who said I was leaving?"

"You said that like you were getting ready to leave, I was gonna see if I can get you to pump my gas first? Those swollen biceps look accustomed to pumping things," she said flirtatiously, making them both smile.

Subsequently, they left the gas station together and went across the street to an Asian family owned restaurant called Supone's, where they got a bit more acquainted as they ate dinner. They flirted with each other every chance they got, so it wasn't a surprise to either of them when their spontaneous date ended with a lingering hug, although Tyree really wanted to taste her delicious looking lips. *Maybe next time* he thought as they released each other. They had no idea when they would see each other again, but they both knew it wouldn't be long.

CHAPTER 22

"What happened last night, ma—you know I was waiting for you to call me back?" Danielle said as she turned off the vacuum, tossing the cord aside.

Erica smiled with her hand on her hip, glancing around the church before replying. "I'm sorry, Danielle. My girl Bubbles took me to her sister's house, and we got faded as fuck. I didn't check my phone until this morning."

"You could have texted me back or something," said Danielle.

"Girl, I was too fucked up to do anything," Erica said, grinning. "I promise you I don't know what kind of weed that was, but it had my ass in another world."

Danielle seemed to soften up as she thought about it, she was anxious to say what was on her mind. "Girl, guess who showed up at my house last night bragging about some guy she'd just met?"

"Who?"

"Your girl Miss Willa," Danielle said as if she still couldn't believe it. "I'm talking about the woman was exuberant; just smiling and shaking her lil' hips. I don't think I've ever seen her that happy before, I was tempted to ask her if she gave him some."

"Shit, that's good for her," Erica said as she smacked her lips. "Hopefully he did tighten her up whoever he is. If not, he needs to so she can move on."

"Don't lie to yourself, ma," Danielle said after smacking her lips. "You know damn well that lowdown scoundrel hasn't moved on either. Just 'cause he doin' you don't mean he's over her, you can lie to yourself if you want to."

"Oh, he's over her, believe that," Erica said with confidence. "He just need her punkass to return to this motherfuckin' church so all the people who left will come back."

Danielle knew her friend was in denial and figured arguing about it was a waste of time. "Ma, let me go ahead and finish vacuuming this floor. I might leave early today 'cause I got some business to take care of. I just wanted to let you know what's going on with your best friend Miss Willa," she said, laughing.

"That bitch ain't my motherfuckin' friend," the teen replied. "I'll talk to you later. I'ma go ahead and let you handle your business, make sure you get that spot over there," she joked.

"I got this, so don't worry about me," Danielle told her. "Just focus on keeping your business straight."

"I promise you I'll be alright," Erica shot back as she headed toward the pastor's office.

The church was a job they both enjoyed. It was easy and allowed them flexibility—they had no idea it's future was coming to an end.

UNGODLY

It was after 10PM when Pastor Armstrong finally shut his eyes after loathing for hours. His fingers were clasped tightly behind his head as he lie in bed, waiting for his wife to return home after noticing how late she stayed out the night before.

He was bothered by the thought she'd moved on with her life, especially since they both were still living under the same roof. He couldn't understand why he was having such a difficult time getting over her. He didn't exactly keep tabs on her whereabouts, but he instinctively kept track of her coming and going—he just wanted to be sure that she was safe.

He was also concerned about her being home at a decent hour after nightfall, and in her bedroom alone, because he was holding out hope they'd get back together. Thus far, she hadn't yet returned to the church as rumors had it, but fortunately for the church, there was an influx of new members in its congregation, for reasons unknown but were appreciated—a blessing in disguise that helped it to stay afloat.

Pastor Armstrong had been lying there contemplating swallowing a handful of sleeping pills that would have more than likely stopped his heart from beating, but fortunately for him, he fell asleep first.

CHAPTER 23

Erica was bored as she sat waiting inside her car in the Walmart parking lot. She brought her friend Bubbles to get some photos copied and was steadily growing impatient when one of her co-workers exited the store, swinging her hips. "Uh-uh, I know this ain't that bitch?" she said as she grabbed the door's handle, wondering who the young male was that she had in tow. *I don't know why this bitch is so weird to me* she thought. The thought to duck crossed her mind to avoid being seen, but instinctively, she pulled on the handle, nudging the door open. "Hey, Ne-Ne, come here!"

Ne-Ne squinted and strained her eyes as she continued to come towards her, pretending as if she didn't recognize her.

"Come here, bitch! Don't try to act like you don't know who this is," Erica said while waving her arm, acting as though she wanted Ne-Ne to quicken her step.

"Hold on, girl. Wait right here," Ne-Ne said to her male friend, who instantly stopped in his tracks and put his hand on his waist. "Erica, is that you?" Ne-Ne said, still playing it off, just a few feet away from the driver's side door.

"Bitch, you know who it is, don't try to play dumb in front of your lil' friend."

"Girl, you know I can barely see," replied Ne-Ne as she inched up to her. "What's up girl, what you doin' comin' to Walmart?"

"I'm waiting for my girl to come out, she had to get some pictures done."

"Printed or copied?"

"I don't know, one of them," said Erica. "I think she had to get some copied."

"My printer at home makes copies just as good as theirs, she could have came to me and saved a few dollars," Ne-Ne said, knowing good and darn well they didn't know where she lived.

"She'll be alright," replied Erica. "Who's the lil' gay boy you got with you?"

"Oh, that's my friend Twan. He's cool," Ne-Ne said before glancing over her shoulder, not wanting him to hear what Erica was saying.

"I don't wanna hold y'all up, I just wanted to say what's up to you. I do need to ask you somethin' though," Erica said as she purposely stayed between her car and the ajarred door. The driver's side window was already stuck when she purchased the car, so she had no choice but to keep the door open.

"What's up?"

"I'm not tryin' to get in your business or nothin' like that, but do you and the pastor got somethin' goin'?"

"What-d' you mean do we got somethin' goin'?" said Ne-Ne with her brows raised.

"If y'all do, it's cool, but I need to know if y'all got somethin' goin'?" the teen repeated.

"Girl, hell nah," Ne-Ne said, offended. "What made you ask me somethin' like that? Are you serious? I can't believe you just asked me that."

"Ne-Ne, you make yourself look suspicious when you wait until everyone else leaves before you go marching into his office. And, if somebody else is around, you and the pastor be acting like y'all don't even know each other, but when y'all are alone, you're the best of friends."

"Girl, hush, all I do is work for that man, just like you," Ne-Ne told her. "Unless the two of you got something going?"

"Nah, never that," Erica lied. "Girl, it ain't no big deal. I was just wondering if y'all had something goin', but if you say no, then it's no. I believe you. I shouldn't have asked you, I'm sorry."

"I feel you, but it's a big deal to me 'cause I don't want nobody thinking no crazy shit like that about me. I can't afford to have rumors like that floating around. I still wanna know why you asked me that. Do you have feelings for him or something?"

"Ne-Ne, let's leave it alone," Erica told her. "I've already told you it ain't nothing like that. I have to be in his office to do my job, but you never come in there while I'm in there, you're only in there when no one else is.

That's what makes it look so suspicious, and it's the only reason why I asked you about it."

"How can you say we talk like the best of friends when no one else is around? You've never heard us talk to be making that kind of statement."

"You're right, but I assume y'all are," Erica told her. "I'm sure you're not just in there sitting around. I'm just saying, it doesn't look right, Ne-Ne."

"Girl, no, it ain't nothin' like that," Ne-Ne assured her. "I had no idea people were thinking like that about me. I will be paying closer attention from now on though."

"Don't worry about it, girl," Erica told her. "I'm glad we had this lil' chat."

"Me too," said Ne-Ne.

"I'ma let y'all get out of here. It looks like your little friend over there is starting to get impatient."

"Let me go ahead and go then," Ne-Ne said while looking over her shoulder. "I guess I'll see you at work tomorrow."

"Alright, girl. Take care."

"You too," Ne-Ne said before walking off.

Erica pulled her door shut and watched Ne-Ne and her friend walk off together. She didn't understand what the two had in common, nor did she care. Erica couldn't quite put her finger on it, but there was something very odd about her co-worker. *Why is this bitch hanging out with a gay boy?*

As soon as Ne-Ne and her friend climbed inside a car, Bubbles startled her when she snatched open the passenger door, immediately handing her an envelope filled with photos. "Girl, what took you so long?"

"Girl, everybody was in there getting pictures done," Bubbles said as she pulled the door shut. "The kiosk line was long as hell."

Erica smiled as she removed the pictures from the envelope and began sifting through them, the conversation she had with Ne-Ne still fresh on her mind. She wasn't for sure, but she felt Ne-Ne hadn't been honest with her—she had no idea what made her feel that way.

Chris parked directly behind the red and white Cadillac Eldorado that filled his mother's driveway, and immediately heard soft music playing in the background when he entered the house. The scent of cherry incense filled his nostrils as soon as he walked through the door—he hoped he hadn't shown up at a bad time.

He didn't want to disturb his mom and her company, so he closed the door lightly behind him before heading toward the living room where the lights were dim. His plan was to surprise them with the delicious looking red velvet cake he'd baked specifically for them, which was no doubt one of his mom's favorites.

As soon as Chris reached the living room, he heard faint moans, which should have served as a warning, then, before he had time to think, he saw the back of Larry Kokane's head looking down toward the floor as he sat in the middle of the living room couch—his mom's head was bobbing up and down like she meant what she was doing. Chris had seen far too many smut videos not to know what she was doing; he couldn't have picked a more fucked up time to show up at her home. "Fuck!" he said under his breath.

He stared with disgust before shutting his eyes. He then began to slowly backpedal down the hallway and nearly tripped.

The thought of his mom giving Larry a blowjob was disturbing to him, but he knew the only person he could blame was himself…

Chris immediately sat the cake down softly on the floor near the front door, then escaped the house with godspeed. It was neither here nor there, but he deeply regretted not making his presence known when he entered the house, he would never make that mistake again.

He climbed inside his car, speeding away from the curb, still bothered by the image he had in his mind.

CHAPTER 24

The choir at Real Love Baptist Church was in the middle of their weekly rehearsal when Pastor Armstrong made an early departure. Everything seemed okay at first, until he was approached by an inquisitive choir member who asked whether or not his wife planned to return—that seemed to spark something inside his soul.

He seemed to get more and more frustrated with each second that passed, which didn't go unnoticed by the choir members.

What they didn't know was that his wife was not home as much as she once was, and whenever she did decide to stay home for the evening, she was constantly on the phone whispering and laughing, the same way they used to do when they first started dating three decades earlier, the pastor was certain he knew the reason for it.

His instincts told him she'd met someone else, and the thought alone was burning a hole in his heart. *Lord, I can't go on like this* he thought as he sped through traffic, not caring about anything other than reaching Erica's apartment. He found his young lover's presence to be quite consoling since he couldn't be with his wife, but Erica was not home when he reached her apartment, nor did she answer the phone when he gave her a ring. "Damn!" he said under his breath.

He returned home and once again considered ending his life as soon as he laid across the bed. The thought of dying became more and more prevalent to him—a recurring thought that he just couldn't seem to shake.

Time seemed to be at a standstill as he painfully awaited his wife's return. Finally, she came stumbling through the door around 2AM, and he figured it would only be a matter of time before she would stop coming home altogether.

The thought made his heart ache even more, and to make matters worse, she had no idea how much she was torturing him.

He fell asleep when his wife went inside her bedroom, just to awake an hour later with a chest full of pain.

He knew that if he couldn't find a way to make the pain subside, he would probably end up dying from a broken heart.

CHAPTER 25

"**I**s it strange or just a coincidence that this bitch decides to take a week vacation a day after I asked her about her and the pastor?" Erica said to Danielle as they headed up the stairs that led to the balcony. "I thought all vacation requests had to be approved first?"

"I don't know, ma. Maybe you spooked her?" Danielle said with uncertainty in her voice. "I wish I could have been there when you asked her about it."

"I don't know why I can't put my finger on it, but something is not right about that bitch," Erica said as they reached the top of the stairs. "It's something I've felt from day one—the bitch makes me itch for some reason."

Danielle was tickled by Erica's comment. She too felt something was not normal about Ne-Ne's demeanor, and it had nothing at all to do with the amount of keys she carried. "It's possible that y'all are both sleeping with the same man, he might be what the two of you have in common?"

"Nah, it's definitely not that," Erica said as they looked over the balcony, she found herself looking toward the pastor's office. "It better not be."

"Ma, you would be amazed at some of the shit that goes on in this crazy world. Shit you wouldn't believe unless you witness it yourself," Danielle said as she sat down on the bench and crossed her legs.

"I already know we live in a crazy world," Erica said as she leaned against the balcony.

"Probably crazier than you think, ma," Danielle said.

The two women locked eyes in a way like they never had before. Erica sensed that her friend was trying to tell her something. "What are you saying?" she said without breaking her stare.

Danielle's eyes were trained on Erica. She thought long and hard before replying. "Ma, can I trust you with a secret?"

Erica crossed her arms as she stared at Danielle, she tried to brace herself mentally for what she was about to hear. "Yeah, what's up?"

"Why are you looking so uncomfortable all of a sudden?" Danielle said without smiling. "You must think I'm about to tell you I like you or something?"

"I don't know. I hope not," Erica said, fidgeting.

"Ah, nah, ma, it's nothing like that," Danielle smiled. "Don't take that the wrong way either. You're a very cool and attractive girl, but I'm not attracted to you like that. I do like you as a friend though."

"Whew, that was close," Erica smiled while wiping her forehead. "I thought you were about to tell me you're in love with me or something."

"Bitch, you wish," Danielle laughed. "Nah, ma, I'm going to tell you something that might fuck you up, but you have to promise me that you won't repeat it."

"I won't, what is it?" the teen said anxiously. "I hope you hurry up and tell me and stop teasing me. You know I wanna know what you're talking about."

"Since I know your secret, I'm going to tell you mine," Danielle said before pausing.

Erica waited for her friend to continue but she sat for a moment just staring at her. "Girl, you better stop playing. I know you're doing all of this procrastinating on purpose. You know I'm dying to hear what you gotta say."

"Alright," Danielle said. "You know how you and Pastor Armstrong has done some creeping?"

"Yeah. I hope you're not about to tell me you fucked with him, too?" Erica asked, frowning.

"No, I'm not about to tell you that, but I can't lie and say I haven't fucked with his wife."

Erica gasped, covering her mouth with her hand. "What? Girl, stop playing; are you serious?"

"As a heart attack."

"Ooooh, not Miss Willa. Oh my god, you're bullshittin', right?" the teen said in disbelief.

"I'm not," Danielle told her. "I knew you probably wouldn't believe me. That's why I said you wouldn't believe some of the stuff that happens in this world. It only happened a few times, but the fact is, we did our thing."

"Oooh-wee, I'm scared of y'all," Erica said, giggling. "I can't believe you sampled some of that old pussy."

"You're sampling old dick, so what's the difference?"

"Oh yeah, I forgot about that," Erica said as she burst out laughing. "I guess I don't have room to be talkin', huh?"

"You sure don't," Danielle said. "It is what it is—we can't take it back."

"Sure can't, nor do I want to," concluded the teen.

She felt closer to Danielle after hearing her secret, but wondered if there were any other secrets she was hiding from her?

They left the church headed in separate directions. Erica's mind was focused on purchasing a bag of weed from the boyfriend of Bubbles' sister, Danielle hoped that she hadn't erred by sharing her secret.

CHAPTER 26

Willa Armstrong was elated to have a man half her age. She had forgotten what it felt like to be infatuated—she did nothing but smile when she and Tyree were in company of each other.

It also excited her to feel like she'd gotten her groove back. She was impressed by her young lover's prowess. It was baffling to her how a man so young could be so highly skilled with his dick and tongue.

Tyree Marshall knew exactly how to console her when she needed comforting; cater to her needs when she was in his presence, and he complimented her constantly about her beauty—literally bringing her to tears, seemingly making her heart melt with each word he spoke.

It felt like it had been forever since anyone had made her feel so special—she was really becoming emotionally attached to her new beau.

She loved how wonderful he made her feel inside and was more than pleased with his sensual lovemaking—what he had inside his pants was the icing on the cake.

Tyree took his time when it came to pleasing her. He made sure that the experience continued to linger inside her mind and loins, long after the physical act was over, which seemed to work like a charm, bringing her back for more. He seemed to appreciate everything about Willa's physique; the fullness; softness; and sweetness when he tasted her, placing his hands, mouth and groin in all the right places, which never failed to result in an earth-shattering orgasm.

The two sat cuddling in a corner in the rear of a movie theater. They fed each other popcorn, one kernel at a time, as they watched a movie about a female serial killer who castrated her male victims and kept their genitals as trophies inside a jar.

The lovebirds were more into each other than they were the movie, so it wasn't a surprise to Willa Armstrong when her young lover's warm-moist lips made contact with her delicate skin, sending chills through her body like an electric shock. He sucked her earlobe inside his mouth before kissing her neck, then slid his large hand, slowly but firmly up and down her thigh, then eased it smoothly between her legs.

"Oooh," she said while shifting her pelvis forward, wanting his experienced fingers to press harder when they grazed her crotch. She was more than receptive to her young lover's touch—she shut her eyes tightly when his large hand made its way inside her panties, causing her juices to flow rapidly as his thick middle finger made its way inside of her moist tunnel, forcing her to spread her legs even farther apart.

"Damn, you're wet," Tyree said as he perforated her warm hole with his long finger.

"Ooooh, that feels good," the older woman said as her super wet vagina tightened around his finger, secreting waves and waves of milky-white fluid which literally robbed her of her energy as it flowed from her body.

Tyree pulled his liquid covered finger from her hot sweet vagina and spread it slowly and evenly across her succulent bottom lip, and then leaned in toward her and sucked it off. "Mmm, that tastes good," he said before kissing her passionately, eagerly gorging the sweet whitish-clear nectar from her bottom lip. He loved how she allowed him to have his way with her—he found her submissive nature to be one of her best qualities. "I'm ready when you are," he said while breathing heavily.

"Ready for what?" she said while pulling away, assuming he was hinting at them having intercourse inside the movie theater.

"To take our relationship to the next level," he said without wavering, then kissed her face and neck in several spots.

"And how do you suppose we do that?"

"I want you to move in with me, Willa. I don't want you to be around your ex anymore."

She was surprised by his bluntness but didn't offer a reply. They barely even knew each other—the thought of moving in with him had never crossed her mind, she was suddenly uncomfortable by his aggressiveness. "Sweetie, I've already told you that you have nothing to worry about."

"Baby, I just don't think that you should be there anymore. It's not right," he said flatly.

"I understand how it must look, especially from the outside, but my soon-to-be-ex-husband and I don't even sleep in the same bed together. We are under the same roof, but I assure you we sleep in two separate bedrooms."

"I get that, baby, but I'm ready for something more permanent," he said as he pulled her closer to him. "I'd love to have you move in with me, Willa."

The preacher's wife felt like she was being pressured. She loved the time she and Tyree spent together, but she wasn't interested at all in being in a serious relationship—the only thing she really wanted was the companionship. She was far from the type who would just sit back and allow herself to be forced into something she was uncomfortable with, so she knew she had to put her foot down. "Look, Tyree, I like you a lot. I really do, but this is something I'll need a little time to think about," she said while staring at him. "I've only lived with one man for the past thirty-five years, and I'm not sure if I'm ready to get used to someone else. At least not yet."

Tyree was shocked but understood where she was coming from. Never once did he consider being rejected by his new prospect, so he began to wonder who she thought was more important. "Well, who do you have feelings for, me or him?"

"Of course my heart is with you, Tyree," she began. "You're the man in my life now. The one I care about but being where I am is familiar to me. Where I am is my comfort zone—the only safe haven I've known for thirty-five years," she continued. "I'm not saying I'll never move in with you. I'm just saying I need more time."

"I understand, baby. There's no rush," he said as he caressed her cheek. "Take however much time you need, it's a standing offer so it'll still be on the table whenever you're ready to accept it."

"Thank you for being understanding, honey," she said, smiling. "You have no idea how amazing I think you are."

"You're pretty amazing yourself," he said before kissing her gently. "That's why I'm so ready to take it to another level."

"We will, sweetie. Just be patient," she said sincerely.

The movie was ending as they finished talking. Everyone began flooding the aisles to make their exit, so they remained in their seats to avoid being trampled. The Eclipse Theater closed its doors for the evening, but Willa and her beau were just getting started. As soon as they climbed inside his truck, they finished what they'd started inside the movie theater, this time it was Willa who started it by unzipping his pants and taking him inside her mouth—they ended the night with multiple orgasms.

Valarie and Larry had just pulled into the parking lot of the J and J apartments when her cell phone indicated that she'd gotten a text message.

"That's probably your son again," Larry said as he parked in a spot beside the front office.

"It is," she said when she looked at her phone, then shook her head as she rang him back.

Chris answered the phone with an attitude. "Damn, mom, it's about damn time!"

"What is it, Chris?" she said when she heard the anger in his voice. She'd become fed up with him acting like he was her guardian—she felt like she didn't have any room to breathe.

"What is it?" he replied angrily. "That's all you can say after I've been calling and texting you all day? I didn't know whether you were dead or alive, but I guess that doesn't matter to you, huh? You could have at least texted me back and said I'm okay."

"I'm okay, Chris," his mom said. "I'm sorry but I've been too busy to call you back before now."

"Where are you?"

"Somewhere safe."

"Somewhere safe?" he repeated. "Oh, now I can't know where you are? Mom, since when did we start keeping secrets from each other?"

Valarie was exhausted after spending a long adventurous day with Larry on the River Mountain Loop Trail at Red Rock Canyon. Her energy level was beyond depleted, plus she was sick and tired of her son treating her like he was her babysitter. "Grow up, Chris," she said in a serious tone. "I'm a grown ass woman and can do whatever I want whenever I want, I don't have to explain anything to you or anyone else."

"Are you serious, mom? Really?" he said as if his feelings were hurt.

"You're not my man, Chris. You're my son," she told him. "Stop thinking I'm obligated to tell you where I am or where I'm going. You might do that with your lil' girlfriend, but don't do it with me," she said with authority.

Chris thought about mentioning the indecent behavior he witnessed a few days prior when he stopped by her house, but he didn't want her to know he'd witnessed it. "Okay, mom, I was just worried about you, that's all," he said in a much calmer voice. "I know now that you're okay, so I'ma let you go. Sorry for bothering you...I'll call you tomorrow," he said before hanging up.

Larry wrapped his arm around his woman when she hung up the phone. He was proud she had finally stood up for herself, it was something that he felt was long overdue. "You look tired, baby," he said before kissing her on the head.

"I am. Very."

"Me too," he whispered. "I don't think you should be out here driving tonight. Camp out at my place and go home in the morning."

Valarie consented by nodding her head. They proceeded to unload the car and hurriedly dragged their belongings to the front door of Larry's apartment, then dropped it in a corner of his living room. It had been a long joyous day filled with hiking, picnicking, drinking champagne and taking a variety of photos—the only thing they wanted now was to get some rest.

The couple stripped down naked and took a quick shower before laying across the bed. A few moments later they were sound asleep.

CHAPTER 27

It hadn't been long since Lisa Miles woke up from a drug-induced stupor when her daughter stopped by to pay her a visit. The visit had not been expected, but it wasn't often that they saw each other, so she wanted to make it count whenever they crossed paths. She observed her now adult daughter standing quietly in the center of the living room, looking around the apartment that she'd grown up in as if everything around her seemed foreign to her. "Baby, you miss being at home, don't you?"

Erica closed her eyes, lowering her chin to her chest, then she opened her eyes and looked at her mom. "I miss you, mama, but I wouldn't necessarily say I miss this apartment." She eased forward, sliding open the closet door between the kitchen and living room. The closet had been designed to house a washer and dryer, but, for Erica, it was a place that held a lot of secrets and painful memories; unfortunately, it was the insidious place she unwillingly lost her virginity to one of her mom's ex-boyfriends when she was ten years old—the molestation continued until she was twelve.

She vividly remembered how her mom didn't believe her after it happened—it was the main reason why their relationship started to crumble, and the sole reason behind her promiscuity.

Erica vaguely recalled mostly all of the accounts of the unwanted assaults; how the man she once trusted and called her stepdad used to force himself on her, holding her down on the ground while forcefully prying her legs apart as he covered her mouth with his hand, making sure she wasn't able to scream for help. She could still remember the muffed grunts he made when he forced himself inside her virgin vagina, and how his musty out-of-shape body dripped with sweat as he pummeled in and out of her repeatedly with his tiny tool, and once he was finished, he left her lying on the floor like a worn-out doormat. He would threaten to kill her and her mom if she ever told anyone, so she made it a habit to just clean herself up once he did his deed and pretended as though nothing had ever happened.

Lisa had oftentimes been inside the next room, less than twenty feet away while Erica was being molested, but not once did she ever come to her daughter's rescue.

Erica was never sure whether or not her mom knew or heard what was happening to her, but even if she had, she was probably too high or spaced out to care, she thought?

Lisa was proud as she watched her daughter, knowing that she was going to make something of herself. She was glad to see that the child she'd birthed had grown up to be a remarkable young woman, despite the many trials and tribulations it took to get her there. She was just about to give Erica a compliment when she saw the tears streaming down both sides of her face. "What's wrong, baby?" she said as she approached her and wrapped her arms around her—she had no idea what was going on.

"Nothing," Erica said as she slid the closet door shut, then used her shoulder to wipe the tears from her face.

Lisa didn't have the slightest idea that the closet she only used as a storage area had been used to rape her daughter repeatedly by a man she'd brought inside the home. A man she once loved and believed she would be with forever, until he upped and left her for her best friend Ebony, who happened to be the mother of two young girls—she hadn't seen or heard a peep from any of them since.

"What's wrong, Erica, why are you crying?" she asked sincerely.

"Nothing's wrong, mama, I just can't believe I was born and raised in this apartment, now I'm fortunate enough to have my own," she lied quickly, not wanting to rehash the memories she thought was behind her. Memories that were old but still extremely painful—there was no doubt in her mind that they would be there forever—the wounds were much too deep to be healed with time, and she didn't want her mother to suffer with her.

Erica knew before, during and after she was molested that her mom was only interested in finding her next hit of crack, so even if she did pose the question and ask why she didn't protect her, she assumed her mom would deny the allegations like she did in the past, making it seem like what happened was somehow her fault. Years after the molestation ended, Erica found it in her heart and forgave her mom, and not once did the subject ever again resurface. The pain she endured was one of her worst kept secrets, but she knew it was time to let it all go.

"Yes, you do have your own apartment, thanks to the pastor and his wife," her mom said. "I'm so blessed to have friends like them. They have been there for me from day one."

"They might need somebody to be there for them now," Erica said as she looked at her mom. "You know they're going through a divorce, right?"

"No, I didn't know that. What happened?" she said, concerned.

"I don't know the details, but they separated some months back."

"Separated? Wow. I didn't know any of that," Lisa said, astounded. "Those two have been together for as long as I can remember. I can't even imagine them not being together. Are they still in the house on Madison?"

"Yep, but sleeping in separate bedrooms."

"Now I know that has to be uncomfortable," Lisa uttered. "I might have to tell Miss Willa to come stay with me until she can get on her feet. I had no idea all of that was happening."

"Probably because you're always somewhere getting high," Erica said as she walked across the living room and sat on the arm of the couch. "I'm sure there's a lot you don't know about."

"Believe me I'm aware of a lot of things," Lisa told her. "Probably a lot more than you think."

Erica didn't know what she meant by that but hoped it didn't mean what she thought it meant. She wanted her relations between her and Pastor Armstrong to remain a secret, so she prayed it wasn't what her mom was hinting at? "And what's that supposed to mean?"

"You still got your job at the church, don't you?"

"Oh yeah, I'm still working," Erica said gallantly. "As far as I know everything is good. Miss Willa don't go no more though."

"What?" Lisa said in disbelief. "Yeah, that really doesn't sound like the Willa I know. Something is definitely wrong if she stopped going to church. I gotta get over there to check on her. I might go ahead and do it today."

You need to instead of chasing that dope Erica thought. "For somebody who claims to know a lot, you sure didn't know about any of this."

"I said I know a lot of things, not everything," Lisa said in her own defense.

"When are you gonna leave them drugs alone, mama? Aren't you tired of getting high?"

"There you go puttin' your nose in grown folks business."

"I'm just sayin', you should be tired of it by now."

"Girl, why are you saying that like I'm out here strung out or something? I'm what you call a functioning addict. You said that like I'm down and out," she said before pausing. "I smoke my lil' dope, but I've always taken good care of myself," she continued. "I keep my own place, my own car, I bathe every day—put on clean clothes, and you know I've always kept food in our bellies. Let's be real about it, I do a lil' dope, but I do no slackin' when it comes to handling my business."

"You're on section 8 though, your rent ain't nothin' but a few dollars."

"Lil' girl, I don't give a shit how much it is as long as it gets paid every month, right?"

"I guess," Erica said with a sigh. "How long do you think you're gonna keep beating the system though?"

"How am I beating the system, Miss motherfuckin'-know-it-all?" Lisa said, putting her hand on her hip.

"Because I'm eighteen now and don't live here anymore. You're not supposed to still be on section 8, receiving food stamps. Somebody somewhere has slipped up, and it's only a matter of time before they figure it out."

"You must gon' tell on me?"

"No," Erica smiled.

"Then I'm not worried about it," her mom said. "I'll deal with it when the time comes."

"It'll be too late by then," Erica interjected.

"I doubt it," her mom said. "I'll get it done when it's time to get it done. The same way I keep my car running right and keep gas in the tank and everything else I do for me. If there's a will there's a way, believe me when I tell you your mom is a survivor."

"Oh, I know," the teen admitted. "You've been making it happen my whole life, and you best believe your daughter is a survivor too. I guess I must have gotten it from you?" she said, smiling.

"I know that's right," said Lisa. "So, what do you plan on doing today?"

"I really don't have plans to do anything."

"I'm glad you finally stopped by to visit me. You're over this way every day, but you hardly ever stop by to visit your mama."

"How would you know when you're never here?" said Erica. "That's the same way it was when I was living here."

"I know, baby, I'm just playing. We might as well go get something to eat since you're here. You got some money?"

"I do, and you know I always got a taste for some hot wings or somethin'," said Erica. "We can go right around the corner to the Wing Stop."

"Why not Mario's?"

"I like the Wing Stop better; it be too many people at Mario's."

"Too many of the wrong people at that. You know somebody might break out and start shooting at any moment," Lisa said while grabbing her purse.

Erica smiled to herself but didn't say anything. She knew exactly what her mom was talking about—the two went out and had a great lunch together. They reminisced about old times—it had been quite some time since they'd had a mother/daughter outing—they found themselves really enjoying each other, they promised to do it again soon.

CHAPTER 28

It was a quarter to ten when Lisa miles rang the doorbell at the Armstrong residence. Miss Willa had been heavy on her mind since the day before so she made it a priority to go see about her. She got no response from her initial ring. She rang the doorbell again after a few minutes had lapsed, then went over to the window to take a look inside.

"Girl, what could you possibly want this early in the morning?" Miss Willa said when she snatched the door open, then unlocked the screen door to let Lisa inside.

"Hey girl, don't tell me you were still gettin' your beauty rest?" Lisa said as she entered the house, allowing the screen door to shut hard behind her.

"I was—I'm up now," Willa said with her hand on her hip, still wearing her pajamas with her hair unkempt. "I was literally just getting out of bed when you rang the doorbell the second time. I'm sorry I didn't have time to get myself together."

"Girl, hush," Lisa said with a smile. "Your looks ain't bothering me. You know I've seen you a lot worse."

Willa smiled as she looked away, exhaling softly to make sure her breath wasn't too offensive.

"It's been a while so I'm just stopping by to see how things are?"

"I'm okay," Miss Willa said with confidence. "I'm sure you've heard by now that Buddy and I are getting a divorce?"

"I just found out about it yesterday," Lisa said with dismay. "He's not here now, is he?" she whispered.

"Nah, he's at the church," said Willa. "At least I think that's where he's at. I really don't care."

"Is he still living here with you?"

"Yeah, we're still here, at least for now," Willa said as she strode across the living room and sat on the edge of a plastic covered sofa. "He sleeps in his bedroom and I sleep in mine."

Lisa allowed the information to sink in before speaking. "Isn't that uncomfortable to know that he's right in the next room?"

"You would think that it would be, but for us, it's not," Miss Willa told her. "Buddy and I have a good understanding. We get along great by not talking to each other—he do his thing and I do mine."

"Any chance of reconciliation?"

"Oh, he'd love that, but it's not happening," Miss Willa said while nodding her head.

"You're saying it's over?"

"It is," she nodded.

"You two have always been so close though; I'm scared to even ask what happened."

"It don't matter, it's over and done," Miss Willa told her. "We both just have to move on with our lives." She didn't reveal to Lisa that Erica was the reason behind their breakup. She was still struggling to put everything behind her and was unbelievably content with the way everything unfolded. She had grown weary of being committed to the same man day after day, week after week, month after month, and year after year, for thirty-eight long agonizing years. She was tired of having to pretend to be perfect, knowing nothing could have been farther from the truth.

To her, it was challenging enough just being a wife, but being a pastor's wife was both debilitating and exhausting. The public had to perceive her as being infallible, but she knew good and darn well that wasn't the case. Mrs. Willa Armstrong was far from perfect, and no one knew that better than her.

"You say it's not uncomfortable staying here with Buddy, but if you ever change your mind, you know you're always welcome to come stay with me. At least until you get on your feet."

"I know, girl, and I appreciate the offer," Miss Willa said sincerely. "Thank you, but they say don't fix nothin' that ain't broken."

"If you say so," said Lisa. "I just wanted to come check on you."

"Well, I sure appreciate you doin' that, but I'm alright. I wouldn't still be here if I wasn't," Miss Willa told her. "My new man asked me to come live with him too."

"Your new man?"

Miss Willa smiled while batting her eyes. "Why do you look so surprised?"

"Willa, I just can't imagine you with someone else. Wow," said Lisa. "Are you gonna move in with him?"

"I'm chewin' on the idea, but I don't know yet."

"Wow," Lisa said again. "You give me hope, at least now I know we're not too old."

They both laughed.

"You know we can't never give up on possibilities. We may be older women, but we're still fine. I know I am," she said, sounding narcissistic. "He's thirteen years my junior and can barely keep up."

Lisa was surprised and was unsure how to respond. "What kind of work does this young man do?"

"He currently drives for Uber but is looking into starting his own ride-sharing company."

"A future CEO?"

"That's right, girl," said Miss Willa.

"Maybe one day I'll get a chance to meet him. Could he be someone you might end up marrying?"

"No, I doubt it," Miss Willa said. "I don't see myself ever getting married again once this divorce is final. My focus now is to have fun."

"What's this new guy's name?"

Miss Willa was hesitant, then said, "Tyree."

"Nice name. He sounds young," said Lisa. "What if Tyree wants to marry you someday, you wouldn't marry him?"

"Not in this lifetime," Willa told her. "I don't think he wants to get married either. It's too soon for us to be having those kind of thoughts, I know he can't seem to get enough of me though."

Lisa laughed at her friend's candidness; she seemed elated to have her groove back. "Is he playing or is he driving that uber?"

Miss Willa burst out laughing, stopping to add, "I'm riding it and he's driving it—he rocks my world—when we're together, we don't do no playing!"

Lisa was speechless—she suddenly decided to change the subject. "Alright girl, if you change your mind about staying here and you don't wanna move in with your new man, don't forget you can stay at my place. I'm hardly ever there, so it'll be almost like having your own apartment."

"I really appreciate it, Lisa, and I'll keep you in mind."

"Do that," said Lisa. "It's time I go ahead and get out of here. I'ma let you go ahead and do something with your hair."

"Girl, forget you."

Lisa smiled while heading toward the front door, she was glad she decided to pay Miss Willa a visit. "Whatever you do, don't ever let your new man see you with your hair undone, he might not be able to handle it."

Willa giggled at Lisa's comment. She knew her friend had a good heart, but because of her losing her battle with drugs, she knew that she'd never take her up on her offer. "My carpet match my drapes," Miss Willa told her. "In other words, I got the same hair down there as I got on my head. Tyree has not given me one complaint."

"Oooh, I'm scared of you."

"I would be too," replied Miss Willa. "Thanks for stopping by and showing your concern. God bless you and have a good day."

"You too," said Lisa.

Miss Willa smiled as she closed the door. She knew she wouldn't be able to go back to sleep, so she showered, got dressed and pulled her cell phone from its charger.

"I know this ain't who I think it is?" Larry said when he answered the phone. He was sitting at the front desk of the J and J apartments, drinking coffee and reading the newspaper.

"It sure is," responded Willa, knowing he'd seen her name on his caller ID. "I hope I didn't catch you at a bad time?"

"Now is as good a time as any, Miss Willa. What can I do for you?" he said as he laid the paper on the counter. "Not saying that you are but I got an apartment for you if you're looking to rent one."

Willa giggled at his joke. She'd always known him to have a sense of humor—he seemed to still be the same ol' Larry he's always been. "No, unfortunately I'm not," she told him. "If I was, it wouldn't be over there because I probably wouldn't be able to keep you away from my door."

"You might have a point," he said, smiling. "How you been doin', Miss Willa. How has life been treating you lately?"

"I have no complaints, Larry. God is good."

"All the time."

"How have you been, Larry, have you been staying out of trouble?"

"I have," he said. "I can't say it's been easy, but somehow I've been managing to do it. Like you said, 'God is good'."

"That's right," she said proudly. "Keep on doin' whatever it is you're doin', 'cause whatever it is it seems to be working."

"I hear you, Miss Willa; I told you I'm not the man I used to be."

"I commend you for striving to be a better you, positive change is always good."

"Positive change is the only kind I plan to make, anything else would be uncivilized," he said as he glanced at his watch. He knew Willa hadn't called him just to be calling—he was just about to ask her about it when she began speaking.

"Larry, does that young girl still live over there?"

"Who, Erica?"

"Yes."

"Yeah, she's still over here, unfortunately."

"Has Buddy's car been over there lately?"

"Every day," he said quickly. "The visiting hasn't slowed down if that's what you're wondering."

"That's all I wanted to know, Larry. Thank you." She didn't know why it mattered to her, but hearing the news still hurt her heart.

"No problem, Miss Willa. Anytime. I hope you have a nice day."

"Thank you, I hope you have a good one as well," she said before hanging up. The thought crossed her mind to go over to the church to confront her soon-to-be ex-husband and his young mistress, but she made arrangements to have breakfast with Tyree instead.

Erica had just left Pastor Armstrong's office when she saw Danielle kneeling on the floor on the opposite side of the church, she appeared to be scraping something off the carpet. "Hey you," she said when she approached her.

"What's up, ma," Danielle said without looking up.

"Is that gum?"

"Yeah," said Danielle. "I don't know why people do this. They're supposed to be church folks, but they'll spit gum on the carpet like they're outside. This stuff is hard as hell to get up too."

"They say if you put ice on it and freeze it, it'll help it come up easier. Too bad we ain't got no ice around here," Erica said while standing almost above her, noticing her jumpsuit wedged nicely between her shapely butt cheeks. "It was probably one of those badass kids?"

"Whoever it was they're out of line," Danielle said, sweating profusely. "Trying to get this shit up is no joke."

"I saw your two-week notice on the pastor's desk," Erica said suddenly. "Why you didn't tell me you're about to quit?"

Danielle stopped what she was doing and looked up at Erica, her eyes appeared to be filling up with tears. "You know I was gon' tell you, ma."

"When?" Erica said with disappointment in her voice.

"I was honestly gon' tell you today—I was just trying to wait until the time was right."

"How long have you been thinking about it, Danielle?"

"Ma, it's not something I wanted to do."

"But you had enough sense to give notice, so you must have been thinking about it for a while."

"Erica, I promise you it wasn't my plan," she said. "I'm just tired of struggling to survive out here."

"Bitch, we're all struggling," Erica told her.

"Not like me," Danielle snapped. "The bank just foreclosed on my house, ma. Right now my realtor is closing on this short sale so I can have the money I need to move back east."

"Dang, I didn't know you was struggling like that," said Erica.

"I know you didn't," Danielle said. "It's been rough for a while now. I haven't paid my mortgage in about six months, ma. I even tried to find a roommate on craigslist to help with the bills, but the girls I meet be wanting to live off me, ain't none of 'em trying to help me pay for nothin'."

"Craigslist? Were you looking for a roommate or a relationship?"

"Honestly, I was looking for anybody who would help me pay my bills, but I did prefer it be a girl. You know how that goes."

"Why you didn't ask me?"

"Ma, I'm not trying to mess up nothin' that you got goin' on. You had to get help yourself, the boss wasn't gon' go for that anyway."

"He don't run me!" Erica said in her own defense. "Girl, you should have told me something. We could have figured this shit out together, we still can."

"I told the pastor a couple months back. He said he couldn't help me."

"I thought that's what churches were for?" Erica said. "If they can help the members of the congregation, they should definitely be able to help their employees."

"Ma, this church shit is all a facade. All of this shit is fake."

"I won't argue with that," the teen said. "I don't think there would be any homeless, or no one going hungry, no loneliness, depression, wars, etcetera, if God and his houses of worship were doing what they're supposed to be doing."

"When I explained to Pastor Armstrong that I was having a hard time paying my mortgage and the rest of my bills, he said he already had too much on his plate, and that he was having difficulties trying to survive himself."

"His old ass didn't tell me nothin' about nothin'," Erica said angrily. "I know he's always stressing about every little thing, but he hasn't said one word to me about you or him struggling financially. I don't know, but I think he's still fucked up about losing his wife."

She finally admitted it Danielle thought. The last discussion they had the teen was in denial. Danielle was grateful to see she'd grown and decided it wasn't worth rehashing. "I wanna go back east anyway, Vegas isn't the place I wanna be anymore."

"It's the only place I know," said Erica. "I'm not too crazy about it either though. You'll keep in touch with me when you leave, right?"

"Of course," Danielle said. "My number ain't gon' change."

"I'ma miss you, girl," Erica said, sadly. "I'ma miss hangin' out with you on and off the job."

"I'ma miss you too, ma, but I'm not gone yet. We still got at least another week to hang out. Besides, you'll still have Ne-Ne to kick it with," she said, smiling.

"Imagine that," Erica shot back. "Her ass should be leaving, not you."

Danielle laughed. She saw the pain on the teenager's face, so she knew that she was serious, but she hoped she would embrace Ne-Ne once she was gone. Danielle began to feel sad herself. She hadn't left yet, but already, she was starting to miss the place.

"We definitely gotta kick it before you leave."

"We will, ma. I promise."

They gave each other an awkward stare. Actually, Erica wanted to run up and embrace the woman she'd come to know, but fought hard to keep herself in check, out of fear of being seen as weak. "Let me get back in there to finish my job. I just wanted to come find you after seeing your notice, it tripped me out 'cause it was just sitting on his desk. His old ass didn't say nothin' about it."

Danielle chuckled.

"It ain't funny," said Erica. "I'm tired of him acting so weak and stupid, he keep it up, he'll be losing me next."

Danielle laughed again. This time she couldn't help herself. "Ma, stop playin', you ain't goin' nowhere. You got me all sidetracked. Let me get this shit up, I'll talk to you later."

"Alright, I'll holla," she said before darting off.

She returned to Pastor Armstrong's office and saw him staring at her ass when she walked by his desk so she pushed it out intentionally when she sat down. "Do you plan on coming by this evening?"

"I don't know. Why?" he whispered.

"'Cause I might wanna hang out with Danielle tonight," she said feistily. "I gotta hang out with her before she leaves."

"It's not like she's leaving tonight," he told her.

"So what," she said, then shifted in her seat. "I wanna hang out with her as much as I can, especially now that I know she's leaving."

Pastor Armstrong sat with his shoulders slumped, he knew the teen wasn't finished talking.

"She and I have so much fun when we go out...unlike me and you."

"Go out with her then, but don't compare her to me," he told her. "If you think drinking and shaking your ass is what constitutes fun—young lady, you got a lot to learn."

"Well, you act like you're sad and depressed all the fuckin' time. I'd rather be out there drinkin' and shakin' my ass than be around you," she continued. "You need to stop thinkin' everything is always about you. Whenever we go out we can't do nothin' anyway 'cause you're always scared somebody might see us together. You need to stop being so grumpy and scary."

Pastor Armstrong was shocked by her barrage of words. The verbal assault was a slap in the face; confirmation that he'd made a terrible mistake when he allowed her to get too comfortable with him—now he was being rewarded with blatant disrespect. He couldn't believe she could be so rude and insensitive after all he'd done for her. He actually began to be upset with himself for getting romantically involved with her—he wished there was some kind of way that he could retract it all. "Alright, go ahead and go out with her if you want to. I don't mind," he said nonchalantly.

"I wasn't asking for your permission if that's what you thought," she said boldly. "I just wanted to know if you was coming over so I'd know what kind of plans I need to make."

"Have fun," he told her.

She paused for a bit while looking down at the floor, then looked up at him and said, "Do you have twenty dollars I can borrow until you pay me next week?"

Pastor Armstrong just looked at her. He couldn't believe she'd become so audacious about asking him for things, but he knew he could only blame himself for that.

"Don't worry about it, keep it, I'll be alright," she said before turning around to stuff money she'd counted earlier inside a bag, then jotted down the amount inside a log. She zipped up the bag and dropped it on his desk with the log on top of it and left his office.

Instead of securing the bag of cash inside the safe like he normally did, Pastor Armstrong placed it inside his desk drawer so he could take it to the drop off box after evening services since he wouldn't be going to Erica's apartment.

When he arrived home that evening, he again found himself alone, sad and deeply depressed—he couldn't help but think about eating a bullet.

CHAPTER 29

Tyree Marshall loved performing oral sex on the women he dated, but not nearly as much as he loved receiving it. He sat on the edge of the black leather sofa inside the den of his home with his legs sprawled completely, as Willa sat on her heels stroking his dick with her hand, with his entire scrotum inside her mouth.

Tyree's eyeballs rolled unwillingly to the back of his head as she sucked his balls then his rod like an oral magician—his ten-inch dick disappeared with ease inside her mouth and throat. "Suck it, baby," he said with one hand clinging the arm of the sofa, the other one gripping the back of her head. He pressed her head down to match the thrust of his hips, the pace began slowly but got faster and faster. "Oh, baby, don't stop! Don't stop. Ooooh, baby, I'm coming."

Willa Armstrong had more than forty years of experience of using her mouth to satisfy men. It was her ace-in-the-hole to get a man hooked—the one thing that her soon-to-be ex-husband loved about her. It was something she had a reputation of doing with a great deal of passion—however, she hated the taste of semen, so she ran to the bathroom to spit it out after Tyree shot his load inside her mouth. She momentarily returned to the den and sat beside him.

"I had no idea you were so talented," Tyree said while caressing her shoulder. "It seems like you open up a little more from one day to the next. I want you to give yourself to me completely, Willa. I know for sure now that you've been holding back on me."

Willa smiled as she gave his statement some thought. She was pleased to know of his appreciation of her oral skills, but not once had she ever heard it referred to as talent—it boosted her ego to know he had no complaints. She knew that the rest of his statement was also accurate and was unsure how to explain why she'd been so conservative. "I feel like we're doing too much too soon," she said before pausing. "And to be honest, it's a lot more than I'm comfortable with."

"You're my woman though," declared Tyree. "There should be no such thing as us doing too much."

"But I'm still married," she whispered. "I feel so guilty…because I know better. What we're doing is wrong in the eyes of God."

"Sweetheart, you're in the process of getting a divorce," he said, trying to comfort her. "You shouldn't feel bad about anything we do, it's not your fault that the courts are slow."

"That doesn't make me feel any better, Tyree," she said as she rolled her eyes. "The fact remains that I'm still married, and we really should have waited until my divorce is final."

"C'mon, baby, that's what I'm talking about," said Tyree. "You're letting your past interfere with our future. I care for you, Willa, and I want a future with you. Do you not want a future with me?"

"You know I do," she said softly.

"Then show me."

"I want to, Tyree, but I'm still married," she told him. "I'm sorry but I can't act like I'm free and clear, knowing that I'm still married to another man."

Why think of this now when we've already done everything Tyree thought to himself. He felt like they were talking in circles so he changed his approach—he had to somehow convince her that she belonged to him, and that her focus should be on him and him alone, not the man that she would be leaving behind.

He leaned forward, kissing her softly on the lips, then repeated it more aggressively before sticking his tongue deeply inside her mouth.

"Mmmm," she said as she sucked his tongue. She reciprocated the kiss, then broke it off and smiled while gazing into his eyes.

"Baby, I know that the attitude and frown is just a front," he began slowly. "I want to meet the real Willa Armstrong. The one under the mask. I know she's sweet, soft, delicate, and delicious. I know she's beautiful on the inside and out, and I know she wants and deserves the kind of love that I have to offer. Please, baby, take off the mask and give me a chance."

"Sweetie, I wouldn't be here with you if I wasn't giving you a chance," she said as she rubbed his knee.

"Let me love you and honor you the way I want to, Willa. Let me appreciate you and do right by you. I truly believe I found my soulmate when I found you. Do you think I'm wrong for wanting you completely?"

"No," she whispered.

"I don't either," he told her. "You shouldn't feel bad about anything we do either. Am I wrong for wanting to cherish you?"

"No."

"I adore you so much, Willa. It warms my heart every time we're together, and when we're apart, I yearn for you. Is it possible for us to leave our pasts behind and concentrate on what the future has in store for us?"

Tears rolled down her face as she tried to respond…she heard the sincerity in his voice. The compassion. The warmth. The way he pronounced his words, she had never before been wooed so strongly. "Okay," she whispered as she leaned into him, unable to force herself to say anything more.

"Yeah?"

"Yes," she said again.

"Thank you, Jesus," he said as he squeezed her shoulder. He laid her softly on the floor and removed her clothing, then took his time removing his own before climbing between her legs.

She responded by raising her legs high in the air, wrapping them behind his neck, then reached down and placed his erect penis inside her, allowing him to plunge as deep as he pleased.

Damn! Tyree thought to himself. He loved how it felt being inside of her. He was impressed how a woman her age could be so flexible, and have such an insatiable urge for sex, but it was one of the things he absolutely loved about her. "You are an amazing woman," he said as he delved deeper inside her, knowing she wanted every inch of his aching erection.

"Thank you, sweetie. So are you," she said while breathing harder, then closed her eyes as he sank his submarine deeper and faster into her ocean.

Tyree stayed inside of her after shooting his load. He felt her walls contracting around his member—a feeling so wonderful no words could ever describe. "I would love to be able to wake up to you every morning just like this. It would be great to start and end my day by making love to you, Willa. Are you still considering moving in with me, or will you and I have to get married first?"

She smiled just from hearing him speak of marriage. Getting hitched again was the farthest thing from her mind, and she couldn't believe he was thinking about it. "No, we don't have to get married first," she said as she kissed him gently. "I will move in with you, Tyree, but, we have to first wait until my divorce is final."

"I guess I can wait until then," he smiled. "I don't see it being too much longer."

"Me either," she said. "I'm expecting to hear something any day now."

She reached down, wrapped her hand around his limp penis and slowly began massaging it. Ever so gently she pulled it back and forth until he was fully erect. Then she climbed on top of him and began riding him backwards, allowing him to see her assortment of goodies while the mouth of her vagina blew out his candle.

It was an hour before closing time when Larry Kokane looked at his watch. He had just finished entering a new tenant's lease into the computer when the door to the office suddenly burst open, the chimes were snatched from the ceiling, crashing onto the floor.

"Where's Nino?" the woman said while scanning the room, in search of any movement inside the office.

Larry was shocked by the woman's anger. He had never once seen her upset before, and before now, had considered her to be one of his nicest tenants. "Nino is out in the field, Ms. Marilyn. What's wrong?"

"That no good lying motherfucker," she said as her jowl shook, her innocent looking eyes began to water.

The office manager couldn't help but notice how freely her breasts swung underneath her shirt—he immediately knew that she wasn't wearing a bra. "What's wrong, Ms. Marilyn?" he repeated.

To not lose her composure she could only stare at him, she attempted to say something but stopped herself.

"What's Nino done, Ms. Marilyn?"

"Just tell that lying bastard to come see me whenever you see him or talk to him," she said while swiping at a tear that fell from her eye. "I'm sorry for coming in here like this, Larry, but please tell Nino to come see me."

"I most certainly will, Ms. Marilyn. Did you call his phone?"

"He ain't answering," she said quickly, appearing to get upset all over again.

"Is there anything I can do for you?"

"No, just tell him what I said," she said, then turned and left.

Five minutes after Ms. Marilyn made her exit, Nino came strolling into the office, looking down at the chimes that laid on the floor next to the door. "Damn, what happened here?" he said to his boss who sat behind the counter, looking directly at him.

"That's why I sent you the text message. Things would be a lot worse if you'd strolled in here five minutes ago."

"What happened?" Nino asked again.

"Man, what's going on with you and Ms. Marilyn?" he said suddenly. "She came looking for you and damn near tore that door down."

"That's who did this?" Nino said, pointing down at the chimes. "That crazy bitch tore these bells down like this?"

"The door did it when she rammed it open," explained the office manager. "What the hell did you do to that woman, Nino?"

"I told her I was gonna stop by today on my lunch break. Something else came up that was more important."

"Stop by for what; I didn't see a work order for her apartment?"

Nino stared at the floor just nodding his head, too embarrassed to make eye contact with his supervisor. He knew that he had to tell his boss the truth—something he knew he might end up regretting later. "Remember a while back when I fixed her AC?"

"Some months back, yeah."

"Man, I messed around and spanked those panties. She's been calling and hounding me ever since."

The office manager tried his best not to laugh. It was the last thing he expected his employee to say. "Tell me you're just bullshittin', Nino. You didn't have sex with that lady, did you."

"She tricked me into doin' it and I've been doin' it ever since."

"So, y'all got something romantic goin' on and she came in here trippin' 'cause you didn't go see her?"

"That's all it is," Nino admitted. "I regret messing around with her."

The office manager laughed. "Too late for regrets."

"I can't get this crazy bitch off my back. I swear she remind me of a fatal attraction."

"Bro, you should have at least called her and told her something came up," his boss said. "How hard can that be, you know how emotional women can get at times."

"Man, I didn't know she was gonna turn out to be a stalker. You should hear these messages she left on my phone. You wanna hear 'em?"

"Nah, that's y'all business, I'ma let you deal with that," his boss said. "After all, you are a maintenance man. Fixing things is your calling—although I don't think women were meant to be included, especially on the job."

Nino found no humor in his boss' statement, the only thing he could do was scratch his head.

"You said she tricked you into sleeping with her?"

"She did."

"How?"

Nino vividly recalled the afternoon when he went to Ms. Marilyn's apartment, but he wanted to explain it in as few words as possible.

"How did she go about tricking you, Nino. Did she offer to pay you or somethin'?"

"Nah, it was nothin' like that," Nino began. "She called me into her bedroom, and when I got in there, she was already naked and bent over doggy-style at the edge of the bed."

"So, you went ahead and eased up in it?"

"Of course, 'Kane what man do you know who would pass up an opportunity like that?" Nino said, trying to justify his position.

"Anyone with standards," his boss said bluntly. "That happened before or after you fixed her air conditioner?"

"It was after," said Nino. "I couldn't pass it up after seeing all that ass, 'Kane."

The office manager found it hard to fathom, he hoped his standards never got that low.

"I didn't really have time to standup in it the way I wanted to. I was on the clock, so I made it a quickie. I made up for it afterwards though," Nino bragged.

His boss giggled before replying. "Apparently it was good enough for her. She acts like she's stuck like Chuck."

"If she is, it don't make her my woman," Nino explained. "It was just something that happened. No feelings were supposed to be involved, no strings should be attached, but I did tell her I'd tighten her up whenever she needed it. I shouldn't have told her that though."

"Why not?" asked his boss.

"Because now she done fucked around and got hooked on it. I think she believes we go together or something?"

"You must have put it down 'cause she was mad as a sonofagun when she came in here," his boss said. "I thought somebody was coming in here to rob me at first, then I saw it was her crazy ass. She didn't know it, but I was about to take off running."

Nino laughed.

"You better get on over there before she comes back," his boss told him. "But first you need to put those chimes back up."

Nino felt relieved when he bent over to pick the chimes up from the floor. "I can't believe she came in here looking for me."

"Tell her under no circumstances should she ever come back in here looking for you. We can't have that, Nino. And don't get sexually involved with anymore of my tenants. It's not good for business, and it makes you look very unprofessional."

Nino was too embarrassed to give a reply. He walked over, grabbed a stool from in front of the counter, plucked a screwdriver from his tool belt and reattached the chimes to the ceiling.

Larry Kokane took a swig from a bottle of cognac he kept behind his counter, he turned to it in times like these when he needed to calm his nerves.

"Man, did you know that good sex can turn a docile old woman into a mad woman?" Nino said as he climbed off the stool.

The office manager thought the conversation was over, he was perplexed about Nino bringing it back up. He took another swig before replying, "It all depends on the woman and how long it's been since she had some good sex," he said. "Ms. Marilyn probably hadn't been intimate with anyone for a while? It's like people who've been stuck in prison for years, all they wanna do is fuck when they get out."

"I don't know but her ass flipped the script on me. She went from zero to sixty in less than thirty seconds."

Larry laughed while covering his face with his hands. He could still see the image of Ms. Marilyn's anger when she burst into the office, he wondered what she would have done if Nino had been there?

"You're laughing now but you'll be crying later," Nino said when he sat on top of the stool he'd placed at the counter. "You're the one that's getting married, watch how fast Valarie turn on you."

"Nah, my baby is too sweet for that."

"That's what you think now," said Nino. "Watch when you tie that knot, sweet Valarie is gon' turn into angry-crazy Valarie."

He smiled then said, "I doubt it."

"That's the same thing I thought about Ms. Marilyn, but you see how she came in here today," Nino said, giggling. "They only do it if you lay the pipe right and put that tongue on 'em—my lizard game is off the chain. If Val doesn't start acting crazy, that mean you ain't doin' something right."

"Man, get out of here and go see that woman," Larry said, smiling. He wasn't smiling about Nino's remark. His smile came from visualizing Ms. Marilyn—he was disgusted by the thought of Nino licking on her. "Make sure you tell her not to come to this office again, unless she's coming to pay her rent."

"I'll tell her," Nino said as he walked out the door.

Larry glanced at his watch again then called Valarie. She told him she'd found the perfect wedding dress, and the planning so far was going smooth. He was thrilled when she told him that Chris had volunteered to cater their reception. That meant he would be spending less money—he was always excited about saving a few dollars.

He surprised Valarie by proposing to her while they were on a sight-seeing helicopter ride over the Las Vegas Strip, and once Chris learned of the proposal, he took it upon himself to take on a more active role in his mom and Larry's wedding. Larry was impressed with his soon to be stepson and the fact that he was acting mature, making it obvious to them both that he was more than willing to go above and beyond to make his mom happy. He expressed to her that he knew no one who was more deserving.

Larry was really looking forward to having Chris as his son. He and Valarie would never have children of their own, but since he'd always wanted to be a father, the opportunity had presented itself, so he planned to be the best stepdad anyone could ask for. It didn't bother him at all that Chris was already an adult.

CHAPTER 30

Pastor Armstrong placed his dark blue polyester suit jacket neatly over the back of his office chair and loosened his tie while glancing over at Erica, who was sitting on the corner of his desk, reading a book. "Young lady, why is it every time I see you reading something it's never the Bible?"

"My god this is crazy," Erica said without looking up, showing a great deal of interest in what she was reading.

Pastor Armstrong glanced at her thighs before opening his Bible. He loved the way her skirt clung to her shapely figure—her big pretty legs had become one of his weaknesses.

"Let me ask you this before you get into your scriptures," she said with a disturbed look on her face. She hopped up from the corner of his desk, still staring at the page of the book, she didn't think to pull down her skirt, seemingly unbothered by the traces of cellulite on the back of her thighs.

Pastor Armstrong peered over the rim of his designer reading glasses, placing a finger on the verse he was about to read. "What's wrong?"

"Are you familiar with a slave from the 1800s named Dred Scott?"

Pastor Armstrong let out a defeated sigh. Hearing the name instantly stirred his emotions, he set the Bible on his desk after flipping it shut. "My mom talked about him a lot when I was a child. It deterred me from doing anything to get in trouble with the law once she explained and made it clear to me how the American justice system felt about Black Americans."

"They treated us so wrong back then," said Erica.

"They still do," he said, correcting her. "Did you read the entire article?"

"I did. It's crazy," she said, still in disbelief.

"I keep that book on my shelf as a constant reminder of what we've been through as a people—it's why I try so hard to keep young people out of the system."

Erica sat back down and just stared at him. Something seemed to have come over her. She finally began to understand. "That's why you took me in, you didn't want me to end up in the system?"

"Yes, that's part of it."

"Danielle too, huh?" she asked.

"Ne-Ne, too," he said. "Do you know the majority of blacks don't even know who Dred Scott was? They never even heard of him."

"That's why it's so important to read," said Erica.

"Exactly," the pastor agreed. "I know you just read the story. Did you get the gist of it though?"

"I did and it's troubling," his young lover said. "That's what made me ask you about it."

"Let's see what you learned," he said suddenly. "It's not a test, it's just a discussion."

"Okay," she said.

"Dred Scott was a slave whose white slave master moved him from one state where slavery was legal to Missouri where it wasn't."

Erica interjected, "Yep, and they forced him to keep being a slave even though they were in a state where it was no longer legal."

"You got it," the pastor said, impressed. "Then when he filed a habeas corpus in the Missouri Supreme Court, asking that he be freed from slavery."

"The writ got denied."

"Yes, it did," the pastor nodded. "I believe the judge's name was Roger B. Taney. I'll never forget that name."

"He had the audacity to say that negroes had no rights that white men were bound to respect," Erica said with emphasis.

Hearing the words made the pastor fight off emotions, he nodded his head slowly while staring down at the floor. "…It sent shockwaves through the black communities all over the country—it was a clear indication that the laws in this country were not written to protect us, they're only used to harm us." He paused. "They're only meant to destroy us, and to keep us in bondage."

"You're talking then or now. I'm confused?" the teen said.

"Both," replied the pastor. "Who's to say that Judge Taney and his family weren't slave masters themselves? Why else would a judge issue that kind of ruling?"

The teen shrugged her shoulders.

"It was before my time, but I know it was a precedent case—judges today are still making similar rulings."

"It's sad," the teen said.

"Our history is full of sad stories, some far more severe than Dred Scott."

"Blacks had it so rough back then," the teen whispered.

"Still do," he said with emphasis. "They're not as bold and blatant as they once were, but believe me, not much has changed between then and now. Well, one thing did change."

"What's that?" said Erica.

"Technology," he said, tapping his cell phone with his finger. "We have cameras and social media as witnesses now—they can't get away with as much as they used to."

"It doesn't seem like we had a place in America back then," the teen said, seemingly searching the pastor's face for answers. "Not even the courts stood up for us."

"Being slaves were the only thing we were ever meant to be in this country," the pastor told her. "The courts have never stood up for us, but God has always stood up for us. We just have to keep believing and trusting in him. He's the only one who won't fail us."

Erica didn't agree but kept her thoughts to herself. She did a lot of pleading with God while growing up—praying until her lips needed Chapstick to put a stop to the rapes, and that her mom get off drugs, but she was yet to see the latter prayer be answered. She wondered how difficult it must be for people like Pastor Armstrong who went around preaching to people that God would answer their prayers if they called on him, when she was more than certain that he hadn't even gotten what he asked for yet. The thought crossed her mind to challenge him on what he'd said, but her thoughts were interrupted when someone knocked on the door.

"Come in," Pastor Armstrong said.

Danielle came in smiling with Ne-Ne behind her, her journey as the church's custodian had run its course. "Hey y'all, good morning. Y'all started the party without us, huh?"

"No, we wouldn't do that," Pastor Armstrong said, pretending as though he was happy to see them. "Y'all come on in."

Erica's demeanor changed abruptly; her arms extended fully as she approached her friend. "This is your last day, girl. I'ma miss you. It's not gonna be the same around here without you," she said as they held their embrace.

"You'll be okay, ma. You're strong," Danielle said sincerely. It had only been one week since she'd submitted her notice, and already she'd sold her car, house, furniture, and other belongings—she had more than the amount she needed to move back east—she was finally beginning to feel like she'd be okay. Real Love Baptist Church would soon be put behind her, and although she and Erica would miss each other dearly, they'd both have to find a way to move on.

Erica looked toward the pastor once her embrace ended. "How long will it be before you find her replacement?"

He looked at her smiling, remembering the first time she'd entered his office and how upset she'd gotten when she thought she might be cleaning the church. "Would you like for me to switch you over from accountant to custodian?"

"Nah, I'm cool," she said, shaking her head quickly.

"We won't worry about it now," he said. "We'll tackle it when the time comes, maybe Ne-Ne could double as janitor and maintenance?"

"No I can't—don't be lying on me, unless you gon' pay me for both of 'em?" Ne-Ne said, joking.

"Well ladies, we got Bible study this afternoon and choir rehearsal this evening, so instead of doing anything major today, just do a walk through to make sure everything is in compliance, then how 'bout we get some food and celebrate Danielle's last day?"

All three women were in agreement. They felt the statement alone was worth celebrating.

"Does pizza and chicken sound like a plan?"

"Yes," they all said.

He left the church by himself headed to KFC where he picked up a party pack of extra crispy chicken, the kind he liked best, then to a Pizza Hut that was only a block away. He purchased three pepperoni and cheese pizzas and five two-liter Pepsi then climbed in his car to head back to the church. While leaving the parking lot, his heart suddenly began racing. *"Oh my god,"* he said as he began to hyperventilate, looking over the lens of his gold-rimmed glasses. He saw his wife's car leaving the parking lot of the donut shop across the street—a man sitting beside her in the passenger seat. The pastor's fears had just been confirmed. He'd felt for a while that she'd met someone but thinking it or assuming it was nothing in comparison to actually seeing it. He now knew that it was exactly what he thought it was, and there was absolutely nothing that he could do about it.

He found himself feeling distraught and helpless; wondering how she could so easily move on with her life, putting him completely behind her, when he found it to be so unbearable living without her. He was at war with despair and was losing terribly.

His heart was in shambles as he watched her car pull swiftly into traffic and dart up the street blending in with the rest of the heavy traffic, sharing occupancy with the man he believed had taken his place, and was getting the lovin' that was once his. *Why, Lord?* He accelerated into traffic and continued to gun his car forward in the opposite direction that his wife had traveled.

His first thought was to make a U-turn and follow her to wherever she was going, but since she hadn't seen him, he decided to wait until she got home to confront her, but because they were in the midst of a divorce, did he even have a right to confront her about it, he wondered? Pastor Armstrong's life had turned into a tailspin—everything seemed so confusing.

Ten minutes later he was back at the church. He had been gone for less than thirty minutes, but his mood change was detected immediately upon his arrival. The three employees grabbed the food and drink, leaving him to loathe alone inside his office. The party of three enjoyed Danielle's going away celebration in the main part of the church—the day's Bible study and choir rehearsal were both cancelled.

A small group of Larry and Valarie's closest family and friends sat on both sides of the Little White Wedding Chapel on the Las Vegas Strip, watching and listening intently to the private ceremony as the beautiful couple exchanged vows they'd written themselves. They kept everything sweet and simple, including the colors, which were lavender and white. It was their special day to showcase their love. They wanted none of their surroundings to outshine them.

Valarie's long pretty face was gloating with happiness as her groom kissed her softly on the lips, and for the first time in a long time, Larry Kokane had a look of innocence like no one would have ever expected—his usual sneaky appearance was overshadowed by love. His only intention was to make Valarie happy and proud, and he wanted to sustain it for the rest of their lives.

He and the magnificent Valarie had not simply fallen in love but had grown in love—the kind of union that he had only heard of but had never experienced—words alone couldn't express how overjoyed he was when the priest pronounced them husband and wife.

They were proud newlyweds when they left the alter—blissfully smiling from ear to ear, anticipating all of their tomorrows as they made their way to the exit. Their small cluster of friends and family tossed rice and flowers, using their smartphones as camcorders to capture the moment.

The beloved couple stopped outside the chapel and had their photographer take more beautiful photos before they climbed inside the limo that awaited them. They had come to the chapel as individuals, but were making their departure as one, Mr. and Mrs. Kokane.

The newly joined couple made their way to their reception that was arranged to take place at their son Chris's restaurant, then whisked off into the sunset to the beautiful Bahamas for their honeymoon—they looked forward to spending eternity together, neither had ever been happier.

Making love and cuddling was how Willa and Tyree spent most of their time. She loved having his strong arms wrapped around her as they lay on the couch inside his living room watching Netflix—his warm embrace made her feel so safe and secure, she literally hated it when it was time for her to leave and return to the house on Madison Street—it seemed to become more uncomfortable with each day that passed, she looked forward to the day she'd leave it behind for good.

She pulled up to the house and parked in her usual spot. Hopped out and checked the mailbox, inside was a letter from her attorney. *Finally,* she thought.

Her heart began pounding as she ripped open the envelope and began reading the letter. It was her divorce decree, informing her that her divorce was final. She stuffed the letter back inside the envelope after she finished reading it and could only smile as she climbed back inside her car and turned the ignition. She pulled away from the curb with her phone pressed to her ear.

"Hello."

"Hi, honey," she said, switching him to speakerphone.

"Oh, hey, did you forget something?" Tyree asked.

"No," she said anxiously, fighting to keep her composure. "Guess what I found sitting in my mailbox when I got home?"

He thought about it a moment, then said, "No, really?"

"Yep, my divorce decree. It's finally official. Buddy and I are no longer married."

"That's great, baby. Wow," Tyree responded. "So, when do you plan to move in with me?"

"You sure don't waste any time, do you?" she said, smiling. "How about…"

"I'm waiting," he said, listening intently.

"How does tomorrow sound, or is that too soon?"

"Too soon! Don't be silly," he told her. "I couldn't wait for this day to come. I'm ready for us to start our life together."

"I thought we already have," she said, joking. "I know what you mean, honey, you just want things to be more permanent."

"Exactly. I can't wait," Tyree said. "Will you be packed and ready to go by tomorrow morning?"

"I'll start packing my things as soon as I get back home."

"…I thought you were already at home?"

"No. I'm on my way to the church now to show Buddy this letter. I'm anxious to show him that we're officially over."

Tyree paused, then said, "Baby…that's not your job. Someone is getting paid to make sure he's properly notified."

"My attorney sent mine so he might get one from the court."

"It's not your responsibility, baby," he reiterated.

"I get that, honey, but I don't want him to have to wait though."

Tyree said nothing. He knew that there had to be something more to it.

Willa Armstrong continued, "I also want to tell him that I forgive him before saying goodbye for good; I want our split to be amicable."

"Let me know how it goes," Tyree told her.

"I will, honey. I'll call you later," she said as she came to a stop in front of the church. "I'm here."

"Okay, baby, call me when you leave. I love you."

"Love you too," she said, then hung up.

Hesitantly, she climbed out of the car, feeling her heart rate increase. It sped up even more as she ascended the steps. The moment was bittersweet. She'd climbed these stairs countless times for several decades, but she knew this would be her very last time setting foot on the property.

No one was in sight when she made her entry. She took a couple of deep breaths, straightened her shoulders, lifted her head, made sure she had a firm grip on the envelope she carried in her hand, then headed to her ex-husband's office in a manner as if he was expecting her.

She tried to visualize how he might respond after seeing the document that severed them completely, she was more than certain that he wouldn't be happy about it.

She paused and took a deep breath when she reached the door to his office. Her stomach began tightening as she turned the doorknob; she nearly lost her bowels when she pushed open the door. "Oh-my-god," she said, bringing her hand to her mouth. "You sonofabitch!"

The pastor was caught completely off guard when the door swung open. He was certain he had locked it, his face had extreme embarrassment written all over it when he immediately leapt to his feet, struggling to stuff his fully erect penis back inside his pants, Ne-Ne scrambling to get off her knees in front of him.

Willa Armstrong stared at him in disgust. "How long has this been goin' on?"

Pastor Armstrong didn't know how to respond. He stood speechless as he zipped up his pants. He appeared to be in shock, deeply regretting he was caught, rolling his eyes at Ne-Ne as if it was all her fault.

"Oh, you don't wanna answer me?" his former wife asked.

His voice was trembling when he responded, he inadvertently looked down at the floor. "Baby, what are you doing here?"

"Don't baby me," she said with her hand on her hip, staring back and forth between him and Ne-Ne. "I can't believe this! I just came to show you these divorce papers—I didn't expect to come across this!"

"It's not what you think, sweetheart," he said without thinking.

"I don't care because I'm not connected to you anymore, but you can't tell me I didn't see what I know I saw," she said after unfolding the papers and waving them in the air in front of him. She looked back and forth between the two and just nodded her head. There was nothing either of them could say to her that would justify their perverted behavior—she was unsure of what to do or say next. "Buddy, I am so astonished. I knew you were a liar and cheater, but I would have never suspected you to be gay," she said as she peered at Ne-Ne, who was smart enough to know not to say anything.

Pastor Armstrong put his head down. He was far too embarrassed to continue speaking.

"I can't believe I came here to show you these papers and you got a man in here sucking you off," she said sternly. "I see I did the right thing by leaving you alone. I didn't mean to come in here and rudely interrupt, go ahead and finish what you two were doing." She turned and left. She was shocked beyond her wildest dreams. She couldn't believe that the man she had given her life to and had been intimate with for more than thirty-five years was messing around with another man. Willa and Buddy were the only ones she knew of at the church who knew Ne-Ne was transgender. Nothing about him resembled a man, and because they respected his right to want to live as a woman—they'd made a promise never to divulge his secret. The woman she'd come to know and respect as Ne-Ne was really Nigel Jackson, and she had no idea that he would ultimately betray her.

She stormed out of her ex-husband's office and went straight home to pack all of her belongings. Tears rolled down her face uncontrollably as she did so, the image she'd seen at the church kept replaying over and over inside her mind.

It really troubled her to witness the man she once loved and adored be sexually involved with another man—she couldn't believe she'd given him more than half of her life. The thought crossed her mind to expose him to the congregation that he loved so much, but since she planned to leave it all behind, that too, would have to be included—she'd leave him to deal with his own demons. It just made her more anxious than ever to move on with her life. She was uninterested in simply turning a page or starting a new chapter, what she really wanted was a new start and in order to get it, she had to close the book. Her moving in with Tyree the following morning was highly anticipated, it would be her way of starting anew.

Nearly six hours after being caught inside his office receiving oral sex from Ne-Ne, Pastor Armstrong showed up at his Madison Street home, reeking of alcohol, and nearly tripped over the packed bags that sat inside on the floor not far from the door. It had been more than two decades since he drank alcohol, and it's a chance that it wouldn't have happened under normal circumstances, but nothing in his life was normal anymore.

At first glance he assumed that the bags were his, but after further inspection, realized they weren't. He held onto the wall, navigating through darkness, as he made his way down the hallway to the old guest room, which was now his bedroom, coming close several times to tumbling over. The overly intoxicated pastor held onto the wall until he found the entrance. He let go and made his way to the bed where he scooted to the head, near the nightstand. He pulled the letter from his pocket that Willa had given him, stared at it intently as he scrunched his eyes, still finding it hard to believe that she was no longer his. *"Fuck!"* he said to himself while rocking back and forth, rubbing his temple. Pastor Armstrong was out of his mind. He continued to think irrationally while sweating profusely, suddenly he reached for the drawer in the nightstand where he kept his pistol. He pulled it out and closed his hand hard around its wooden handle, brandishing it around in the air before placing it near his temple, thinking if he pulled the trigger all of his pain would be over, seemingly unable to shake the evil spirit that had grabbed hold of him. The combination of his deranged thoughts and out-of-control emotions had turned his brain into a pressure cooker, causing the once respected pastor to be dangerously unstable and unpredictable—there was no question he was a danger to himself and everyone around him. He pressed the cold steel muzzle of the loaded firearm hard against his temple but couldn't bring himself to the point to pull the trigger. He then opened his eyes and lowered the muzzle to his mouth wrapping his lips around it; closed his eyes again and began crying once he realized that he just didn't have the balls to pull the trigger. He'd reached the same conclusion each time he considered taking his own life—living life was too painful, yet he couldn't pull the trigger—the pastor of Real Love Baptist Church was discombobulated, but still, couldn't rid himself of the recurring thought of wanting to die.

Suddenly he climbed to his feet, went inside of the bathroom, looked himself in the eye while standing in front of the mirror, then placed the cold hard muzzle back against his head. He was more determined than ever to carry out the act, finding himself becoming more and more irate as he stared at himself, still unable to find the courage that was necessary to pull the trigger.

He began to speak outlandishly and curse himself out, hardly recognizing the person that stared back at him. "You bitch motherfucker," he said through clenched teeth, beads of sweat formed in clusters across his forehead. His eyes were bloodshot as he stared at his reflection. With tears streaming down both sides of his face, he continued to ramble, slipping deeper into despair. "You're a bitch! How the fuck can you call yourself a man when you don't even have the balls to kill yourself?"

The longer Pastor Armstrong faced himself in the mirror, the more he disliked who he'd become. One of his pet peeves was hypocrisy, so he continued his quest of ranting and raving. *Lord, I know you said we shouldn't lean toward our own understanding, but my own understanding is all I have…I love you, Lord, and I ask that you forgive me for what I'm about to do.*

He removed the gun from his head, allowing his arm to fall heavily to his side. With his other hand he grabbed a towel from the towel rack and wiped the sweat from his forehead. He shut his eyes and sighed, made his way out the bathroom before entering the dark hallway, heading straight to Willa's bedroom where she was asleep.

He entered the bedroom swiftly and silently, approached the woman that was once his wife, put the gun near her head and pulled the trigger repeatedly. He stared at her motionless body in awe, trying to recuperate from the deafening gunshots, as large chunks of his late wife's skull and brain matter slid down the headboard. He had no doubts now that his life was over. This time, without thinking, Pastor Buddy Armstrong turned the gun on himself and squeezed the trigger. He had a smile on his face when he hit the floor—all of his troubles and woes were finally behind him, stemming from the fact that he couldn't handle rejection, figuring if he couldn't have Willa, no one could.

The once God-fearing man who'd spent the majority of his life serving the Lord would now spend eternity rotting in hell.

Erica was watching the evening news when she learned of the atrocity. A concerned neighbor had been walking his dog when he heard multiple gunshots ring out inside the Madison Street home—the only thing he knew to do was call 911. Authorities were dispatched to the scene as soon as they received the call, upon arrival a forced entry was made, and the murder-suicide was soon discovered.

Erica was at a loss for words and had no clue what to do next. Tears streamed uncontrollably down both sides of her face as she sat on the edge of the living room couch, thinking about the secret she'd withheld from him—a secret she had wanted to be a surprise.

The now deceased pastor's sixty-third birthday was only a few months away. She was hoping to give him the best gift of his life—for the first time in nearly sixty-three years, Pastor Buddy Armstrong was finally going to be a father.

TERRENCE BROTHERS

Willa and Tyree's future plans were ended before they ever got started—they will never know what their life together would have become.

Truth Publications LLC Presents

UNETHICAL REVISED

CHAPTER 1

On a quiet afternoon in the constantly-evolving city of Las Vegas, Billy Brocks allowed himself a chance to relax as he sunk deeper into the black leather recliner inside the enclosure of his luxurious office. He was enjoying an extravagant lifestyle as a successful criminal-defense attorney, in the place now known as Raider-Nation.

He had just got lost in his thoughts when he was suddenly interrupted by his longtime secretary, Simone, her voice was soft and sensual as it came over the intercom.

"Mr. Brocks, a client is here to see you. Should I send him in, sir?"

"Who is it, Simone?"

"It's Mr. Cooper, sir."

"Yes, send him in, please," he said gratefully.

The dark-stained cherry oakwood door swung open to Mr. Brocks' office, a tall black man quietly entered, a sheepish grin spread across his face. He wore a dark blue tailored Armani suit, a white Los Angeles Dodger's baseball cap with blue letters affixed, and an expensive pair of all white leather loafers. His voice filled the room when he saw his attorney slowly approaching him—he knew that his money was well-spent, "You're the man, Mr. Brocks. You know I wouldn't be here if it wasn't for you."

"That's right, Charles, you owe me one," the dapper attorney said when he walked up to the man and shook his hand.

It just so happened that Charles Cooper was only one of several clients that Mr. Brocks had managed to get released from the Las Vegas county jail the day before. The well-dressed black man had been caught red-handed while driving around town with a loaded firearm in his possession. He was pulled over and arrested after a police officer conducted a random search of his vehicle. He then notified Mr. Brocks, and after a thorough review of the police report, Mr. Brocks filed a motion to the clerk of the Regional Justice Center, alleging that the arresting officer had not had probable cause to pull over nor search Mr. Cooper's vehicle. The officer involved held Mr. Brocks in high respect, so he admitted to the judge at the time of the hearing that Mr. Cooper had not violated any traffic infractions, and that he had only pulled the vehicle over, because his own curiosity had gotten the best of him. The officer said he wondered how a young black man like Mr. Cooper was able to afford a new-model Mercedes Benz. The district court judge ruled that probable cause did not exist, and that Mr. Cooper should not have been pulled over nor searched, just because he was a black man driving a nice vehicle. The judge ordered the case dismissed.

Meanwhile, as the two men stood inside the spacious office, the temperament changed as they both fell silent. Thoughts raced through both of their minds before Mr. Brocks decided to break the silence. "What's next for you, Charles?"

The large black man continued to gaze aimlessly outside the large window of Mr. Brocks' office, then slowly replied, "I don't know, Mr. Brocks. I'm thinking about moving back to LA, but my wife and I think we might stand a better chance of raising our daughter right here in Las Vegas. I haven't decided yet, but hopefully, I'll figure it out before it's too late."

It was a statement that Billy Brocks could definitely relate to. Although he was an attorney living the American Dream, he too, had not yet figured things out. After a few moments of silence, Charles Cooper thanked Mr. Brocks for everything he'd done. He looked him square in the eye as he shook his hand, then turned and left, optimistic that he would never again need his assistance.

Several minutes after Charles Cooper had left his office, Billy Brocks still sat on the corner of his desk, wondering to himself the same thing he'd asked Mr. Cooper, *what's next for you?* It was a question he had been asking himself for the past few years. The answer remained the same. He simply did not know.

Born and raised in Las Vegas on April 18, 1969, Billy Brocks derived from a wealthy Caucasian background. Raised only by his father and grandfather, they were the two men he'd always looked up to. Unfortunately, both men had passed away, but their deaths lingered in his mind as if they were recent, he wondered if he would ever get over it.

Billy Brocks never knew his mother or grandmother. He only knew the awful things he heard about them through his father and grandfather. Edwin Brocks, Sr., had died of a stroke at the age of seventy. Billy was only twenty-five at the time and away at law school when his grandfather passed away. He had only been a few months away from taking his bar exam, so his father decided against telling him about it until after he finished law school and passed the bar exam.

When spring arrived, the young aspiring attorney returned to the fabulous Las Vegas valley just to learn that his grandfather had passed away. Billy couldn't believe it, he could barely hold himself together when he realized he'd never see the wise man alive again. Edwin Brocks, Jr., consoled his son, explaining why he'd felt it was best to wait before telling him about his grandfather's death. Both men had been attorneys themselves, but it was the grandfather who'd dreamed of seeing Billy grow up to become a successful attorney. Billy was the reason why both men had shed blood, sweat, and tears to build Brocks & Brocks Law Offices from the ground up. It was now the most exquisite law firm in Las Vegas, and Billy was finally fulfilling his grandfather's dream, but he was troubled by the fact that the old man wasn't around to witness it.

Edwin Brocks, Jr., was the one who taught Billy everything he needed to know about being a successful attorney. He took Billy to the firm on a daily basis to show him the ropes until his own life suddenly came to an end.

One early Sunday morning, Billy was awakened by the loud ring of the telephone. He was reluctant to answer it at first because he was hoping that his dad would answer it. Besides, it was the weekend and he'd planned to sleep in. After about the fourth ring, he finally reached over toward the nightstand and grabbed the receiver. "Hello."

"Hi, my name is Lisa Rider, I'm a nurse at Valley Hospital. I'm sorry to disturb you, sir, but we have an Edwin Brocks, Jr., here at the hospital, would you happen to know him?"

"Yes, he's my dad. Is he all right?"

The nurse heard the change in Billy's tone after hearing his father's name, so she continued in a caring voice, "I'm sorry, but he's suffering from a rare heart condition, and we're unsure whether or not he's going to make it."

Billy hung up the phone after telling the nurse he'd be there shortly. He quickly climbed out of the king-size bed, then ran down the hallway to his father's bedroom to see if the phone call had been some kind of joke. His thoughts raced rapidly as he ran into the bathroom. His father hadn't been home at all the previous evening, but he hadn't realized it until he checked the bedroom. Billy had known about his father's heart condition, but had never known it to cause his father any problems. He didn't know what to think. He flushed the toilet, but didn't bother wiping up the pee that splashed on the toilet seat. He grabbed a towel, washed his face then brushed his teeth. He rinsed out his mouth, spit the contents inside the sink, then hurried down the hallway toward his bedroom. He wasn't going to work, so he didn't waste time worrying about what color suit or tie he'd wear. He slipped into an old pair of sweat pants, a sweatshirt, and a pair of Nike jogging sneakers, then grabbed his car keys from the nightstand and headed toward the garage door. It was dark when he entered the garage, but it didn't take long for his eyes to adjust to the darkness. He squeezed behind his father's truck and made his way toward the car that was parked at the far end of the four-car garage. He snatched off the cover that had been placed over it.

He got inside the smoky gray BMW and pulled the door shut after he started the engine. He reached up and flipped a switch on the car's sun visor, the garage door immediately began to roll open. Once the door was high enough, Billy pressed down heavily on the gas pedal and was soon at the tip of the driveway waiting to enter the street, when he flipped the switch again the door began descending, he was already halfway up the street by the time it shut. Soon thereafter, he was heading up the freeway ramp.

He turned on the radio as he heavily accelerated the BMW 7 series. He was desperately hoping that his dad would pull through, but tried his best not to think about it. He sped up as he recalled the nurse's tone of voice when she told him they didn't know if his dad would make it. He swerved in and out of traffic as he traveled along the smooth highway, and was suddenly relieved when he finally saw the large red sign flashing Valley Hospital. He began switching lanes in a desperate attempt to make his way toward the highway's exit ramp.

Once inside the hospital's parking lot, he immediately spotted a parking space large enough to hold the BMW. He stepped out of the Beamer, but didn't worry about locking the door. He simply activated the car's alarm by using the remote control on his key ring before running briskly toward the hospital's entrance. As he got closer to the door, he tried to remember the name of the nurse he'd talked to on the phone. He couldn't remember, so as soon as he entered the building, he walked directly to the counter that was closest to the door. An elderly nurse, who worked in ICU, stood up quickly. "May I help you, sir?" she asked softly.

"Yes, ma'am. I received a call from a nurse who works here—I can't recall her name—but she said that my father, Edwin Brocks, Jr., is here at your hospital and I'm wondering if you could tell me where he is?"

"Hold on a minute, sir. Let me check the roster."

As soon as the nurse reached for the roster behind the counter, another nurse had just walked up to remove a name off of it. The two nurses exchanged a few words before the elderly one turned and pointed the younger one in Billy's direction. Billy watched closely as he stood with a concerned look on his face. The younger nurse approached him and shook his hand. "Hi, are you the son of Edwin Brocks?"

"Yes. Is he all right?"

"I'm Lisa Rider, the one who called to inform you of your father's condition. I'm sorry to be the one to tell you this, but your father passed away shortly after you and I talked on the phone."

"What! I don't understand."

"I'm sorry, sir, but he didn't make it."

Billy was sad and confused. He never heard the nurse say she was sorry because he passed out and was stretched across the hospital's floor in a supine position. When he came to shortly thereafter, the nurse was cradling his head in her bosom while fanning his face with her hand. Once he'd fully regained consciousness, Billy was suddenly in a hurry to leave the hospital. He had never expected history to repeat itself, but since it had, he wasn't sure if he would be able to deal with it. He had barely been able to cope when his grandfather died, now he was faced with the fact that his dad was dead too. He no longer had the two men to look up to, but he vowed to always remember the words they instilled in him. They constantly reminded him that women were never to be trusted, which probably explains why neither man had a woman by his side at his time of death.

Billy was staring down at his own life as he sat in his office on the corner of his desk. He had reached all the goals he'd ever set for himself, but was still unhappy feeling that something was missing. He seemed to be following in the same footsteps as his father and grandfather, he wondered, if they too, were as lonely and unhappy as him.

CHAPTER 2

"Flight number 171 from Atlanta to Las Vegas will be leaving in approximately ten minutes. I repeat, flight 171 from Atlanta to Las Vegas will be leaving in approximately ten minutes!"

Crystal Tradwell heard the announcement and slowly rose to her feet. She had been sitting inside the lobby of the Atlanta airport for at least an hour—it was the announcement she had been waiting for. Her feeling of elation immediately turned into regret because the red high-heel pumps she chose to wear had become a real pain. She contemplated changing them before boarding the plane, but quickly decided against it because she didn't think she'd be able to get her bag retagged and still make her flight on time. She desperately wanted to get started on her journey, and although she'd never been to Las Vegas, she was extremely anxious to start her new life, because the ATL had given her too many bad memories. She felt she had been in Georgia for far too long and it was time to do something different with her life.

The product of a biracial relationship, Crystal Tradwell was as thick and sexy as they come. She stood five feet, four inches tall and weighed one hundred and forty pounds—she was well put together without a doubt. Most men found themselves attracted to her, but were often confused about her nationality. A lot of women also drooled over Crystal, and though many were jealous, she didn't let it bother her. Being a mixture of Asian and African American, Crystal's parent's interracial relationship had soured and began to crumble soon after she was born. They'd often used her as an excuse for many of their fights and disagreements until the abuse had eventually turned directly toward her. After several of their nosy neighbors called the police, reporting possible child abuse, the State of Georgia came and removed her from her parent's custody, placing her in foster care. Crystal was diagnosed with attention-deficit disorder at the age of five. Her constant temper tantrums proved to be too much for all her potential substitute families to handle; so she bounced around from one group home after another until she eventually ran away at the age of fourteen. The tough Atlanta streets were like an adventure to her. She had never felt loved, nor did she know how to love, but like a lot of things, hopefully it was something that would develop with time. It didn't take her long at all to realize that her gesture and smile was her key to survival. Many people would stop and stare when she walked down the street—when she heard the yells and chants, she knew they were for her— she'd quietly smile to herself while swaying her hips back and forth.

Crystal was fourteen but still a virgin. She had only kissed a few boys while playing games at school, so she'd earned a reputation of being a tease.

Her first night of being homeless, she was cold and didn't have a clue where her next meal would come from. She wandered around drowsily before stumbling upon a small motel that had a lobby, she entered the building with hopes of finding a sofa or somewhere warm to sleep. The air inside the motel was thick and smelled of mildew, but she didn't let it bother her. She was more concerned with things of more importance, like finding something to fill her empty stomach and a comfortable place to lie down for the night.

"Can I help you, miss?" a man asked in a raspy voice.

Crystal was startled. The voice seemed to be coming from behind the counter, of which she looked, but didn't see anyone. The clerk suddenly made himself visible. He was a skinny white man appearing to be in his mid to late twenties with a few missing teeth and long sideburns. He'd been sitting on a stool behind the counter. "Are you lost, miss?"

"No," Crystal said in a girl-like voice.

"What are you doing in here all by yourself so late at night?"

"Hoping to find something to eat and somewhere to sleep," she answered honestly.

"How old are you, and where are your parents?" the man asked while staring at her.

"I'm sixteen, and I don't have any parents."

The man knew she was lying because she looked nowhere near sixteen, but after looking her over, seeing how well-developed she was, he decided to help her. "Do you have any money?" he asked nicely.

"No," Crystal whispered.

"Well, sweetheart, I can give you something to eat and a room to sleep in for tonight, but I can't do much more than that."

"That'll be cool," she said with a grin.

"My name's Joe. What's yours?"

"Crystal."

"Well, Crystal, that's a pretty name for a pretty girl."

"Thank you."

"Let's go find your room.

The man with the missing teeth grabbed the room key and locked the office door behind him, then led Crystal down a dimly lit hallway. They reached room number 20, which was the last room at the end of the hallway—Joe unlocked the door and showed Crystal around. She thought the man was acting rather strange when he began pointing out obvious things, such as the twin-size bed, the bathroom, and an old thirteen-inch TV set that had no remote control, which he said was only there in case she got bored during the night. Joe told Crystal to make herself at home and that he'd be back with some food in only a few minutes. "You like hamburgers?" he asked.

"Yeah," Crystal answered.

Minutes later, Joe entered the deli next door to the shoddy motel. He grabbed a small bag of Doritos, two ready-made cheeseburgers, a few napkins, and a straw for the large fountain drink he'd made. He handed the clerk a ten-dollar bill and told her to keep the change while he headed toward the exit.

Once back at the motel, Joe's heart began to beat with anticipation. He took something from his small black duffel bag that was behind the counter before heading back down the hallway toward Crystal's room. He knocked softly on the door before announcing his name, but Crystal barely heard it. She was exhausted and had fallen asleep on the bed shortly after he'd left. When she climbed out of bed to open the door, he was standing there glaring down at her, holding up the bag of food he'd bought at the deli. "Here, sweetheart, I got some food here for you," he said while handing her the brown paper bag. "Eat your food and sleep well. I'll see you in the morning."

"Thank you," Crystal replied, then closed the door. She turned on the TV, then climbed on the bed to eat her food. When she swallowed the last bite of her cheeseburger, she placed her lips around the straw, slurping down the last of the ice-cold soda, then turned off the TV and went to bed.

When she woke up the next morning, she didn't understand what happened. Her body was in a tremendous amount of pain, and she slowly began crying after noticing that her clothes had been ripped from her body. Dried blood covered both sides of her inner thighs and was all over the bed where she'd slept.

Crystal was completely dumbfounded as to what happened, having no memory at all of the night before. She climbed out the bed in an attempt to go to the bathroom, but fell to the floor when she tried to walk. Her anus was in pain, and she had no idea what to do. She placed a hand between her ass cheeks, then began to panic when she felt the warm blood streaming through her fingers and down her wrist. The sight of all the blood had been too much for her to handle. She remembered being so horrified that she'd held her breath as she crawled to the bathroom.

Seven years later, she still remember how helpless she felt. She unwillingly lost her virginity to someone who'd brutally raped and sodomized her, and she still wasn't sure who did it or how it happened. She only knew that she was alone when she went to bed that night, although she had suspicions, she was too embarrassed about what happened to tell anyone— she remembered wanting to leave the motel room so badly and just forgetting about the entire night. That night had only been the beginning of the seven years she would have to endure of selling her body to survive. She had been sexually involved with countless men and women since that horrific night. She gained a lot of experience—she didn't just do it all—she did it well.

At the young age of twenty-one, Crystal was in deep thought as the large jetliner left the ground. She'd heard many wonderful stories about Las Vegas, and she only hoped it was everything everyone said it was. She'd saved some money, but now worried that it wasn't enough.

As the plane began its journey across the big blue skies, Crystal closed her eyes and began to think about her new life that lie ahead.

CHAPTER 3

When the plane landed at Las Vegas's McCarran Airport, Crystal was already looking for the exit. She took a short but well-needed nap during the flight; now she was eager to find out what Las Vegas was all about.

She exited the plane, then went to locate her luggage. She only had one medium-size suitcase and two carry-on bags, but it still took her a half an hour to find it. She was really new to this traveling thing, so there were a lot of things she didn't know. It was her first time ever being outside of the State of Georgia, but after reading a few signs and asking for assistance, she managed to learn exactly where to go to find her luggage, as well as where she'd need to go to catch a cab.

She went outside and asked a middle-aged cab driver if he would assist her in finding a reasonably priced motel. She didn't have any money to waste, so she knew that she had to manage it well. The cab driver asked if she'd prefer a room downtown or on the Strip, but she didn't know the difference between the two, so she requested whichever one would be the cheapest.

He recommended Fremont Street, and she accepted, so he opened the door of his cab and allowed her to place her luggage on the backseat.

Minutes after they left the airport's parking lot, Crystal found herself fascinated by the beautiful lights that lined the Las Vegas Strip. She tried her best to see everything on both sides of the street, but couldn't focus too long on anything, because she was also keeping an eye on the cab's meter. She'd saved six thousand dollars, but she knew it would only take her so far. It was Friday night, and she knew she had all weekend to tour as much of the city as possible before going out to look for a job on Monday. The cab driver suddenly interrupted her thoughts when he began to point out different buildings and landmarks as they rode down Las Vegas Boulevard. He wasn't driving fast at all, so she became concerned because the meter was already at eighteen dollars, and they still hadn't reached the downtown motel. "How much farther do we have to go?" she asked nervously.

"Oh, we'll be there in five minutes," he answered calmly, trying to offset the nervousness he heard in her voice. He had been observing her through the cab's rearview mirror ever since they'd left the airport, so he was already aware of how careful she was watching the meter. "Don't worry about the meter, sweetheart. When we get to the motel, just give me whatever you think is fair" he said as he turned off the meter.

Crystal smiled and said, "Thank you."

The remainder of the trip was done in mere silence, but the gorgeous Atlanta native seemed much more relaxed. When they pulled into the parking lot of the downtown motel, she was anxious to get out of the cab—her legs were severely cramped and she desperately wanted to stretch them out. She stretched and shook her legs one at a time, then reached inside her purse and removed twenty-five dollars, then handed it to the cab driver. He smiled graciously while accepting the money, then swiftly stuffed it inside the front pocket of his baggy jeans. "Need help?" he asked nicely.

"Yes, please," Crystal answered.

She grabbed the two carry-on bags and allowed him to grab the heavier suitcase. "Thank you," she said.

"No problem."

The cab driver followed closely behind as Crystal walked toward the motel's front office. He really appreciated the view. He already knew that Crystal was beautiful, but he had no idea she had what he considered to be a perfect body. Not only did she possess a perfectly round ass, but her hips and thighs was also guaranteed to grab any man's attention—the only thing he could think was *goddamn!* When they entered the motel's front office, it seemed that every light inside the building was on. It was extremely bright, and the air inside was cold as they approached the counter.

Crystal sat her luggage on the ground in front of the counter, and thanked the cab driver again as he wished her well in Las Vegas. He already knew in his mind that she would be fine, so he backed toward the door that they entered through, and left her standing by herself at the counter.

She quickly settled into her room and turned on the TV. It was just past eleven p.m., so she flipped through the channels and decided on watching the news. Seeing the anchors were an immediate reminder that she was no longer in Atlanta, and she found herself intrigued by the city of Las Vegas in the background. It was still kind of early, so she decided to take a peek at the

Las Vegas nightlife. She took a quick shower and changed clothes before stuffing a twenty-dollar bill in the back pocket of her tight-fitting designer jeans. She left the room and took a stroll up Fremont Street. She was careful to observe everything in the area to be sure she'd be able to find her way back to her room. With every step she took, she gained more and more confidence and believed that her life in Las Vegas would be just fine.

She looked around and noticed that several people were staring in her direction. *You still got it, girl. This might be a new city, but turning heads is nothing new to you,* she thought to herself. She'd suddenly began to feel at ease. She walked casually inside a nearby gift shop and purchased a baseball cap. She wished she'd pocketed a smaller bill, but she handed the twenty-dollar bill to the gift shop's clerk and waited for her change.

When she stepped outside the gift shop, she put the cap on backwards and continued her stroll up Fremont Street.

She observed everything in her vicinity, including women who looked like prostitutes and men who looked like pimps. Many others appeared to be tourists, but all she thought about at the moment was the life she'd left in Atlanta, Georgia.

Crystal was lost in her thoughts and didn't notice that her pace had quickened, suddenly everything was wiped from her mind when she found herself mesmerized by the beautiful array of lights that shined above her. She smiled as she looked around before being tapped on the shoulder by an elderly woman. "It's called the Fremont Street experience."

She smiled at the woman before replying, "It's beautiful. I'm new in town, and I've never seen anything like this before."

The older woman smiled at Crystal, then went inside a casino. She'd encountered countless people who had been fascinated by the lights of Las Vegas, so she moved on without giving it a second thought. Crystal was not the first, nor would she be the last who would enjoy viewing the colorful lights of the Fremont Street experience.

Crystal stood and watched the lights for another fifteen minutes, then decided that it was time to head back to the motel. She had some loose change in her pocket after buying the baseball cap, so she stopped just inside the doorway of a casino and tried her luck at the slot machines.

It was past midnight, but since the downtown streets were still crowded with people, she decided against rushing back to the motel. She figured Vegas was all about having a good time, so she continued to play the slot machines and drank free cocktails until two in the morning. She became somewhat intoxicated and had lost fourteen dollars, so she knew that it was time to call it a night. She hurried back to her room and smiled as she read a sign on a marquee across the street. It read the Lucky Lady Motel, and although she wasn't feeling too lucky herself after losing fourteen dollars, she felt extremely good about herself and the decision she made to move to Las Vegas to start a new life. She entered her room and closed the door behind her and felt the same sensation that the cab driver had felt. She breathed a sigh of relief, and then laughed out loud, because she had no doubt she would be all right.

CHAPTER 4

Billy was in deep thought while sipping the hot black coffee he'd just purchased from Starbucks. It was early Monday morning, supposedly a fresh start of a new workweek, but already, it was starting off terribly for him. He was upset as he neared the Regional Justice Center. His new secretary, Yvonne, was delinquent in filing a motion that he needed to help one of his clients—now he found himself in a bad spot. He had no doubt that Simone would have gotten it done if she hadn't had a appointment with her gynecologist. Neither here or there, he expected Yvonne to take care of it.

His case involved a female witness who could substantiate his client's alibi defense, but since his office hadn't been able to locate her, he hoped the judge would grant him the extra time he'd need to try to find her. He figured he'd explain the situation to the court, and after hearing his explanation, the judge would be obliged to grant his oral request.

Upon entering the courtroom, Billy's case was called almost immediately after he sat down. He stood and approached the defense table, then nicely explained to the court that his office had in fact prepared a motion for a continuance, but since he'd recently hired a new secretary, she'd failed to file the motion that should have been filed on Friday—that's the reason it wasn't inside the case file to be considered by the court.

"Objection, Your Honor!" the district attorney blurted out. "This case has been pending inside this courtroom for six months now, and the State is prepared to prosecute. Mr. Brocks' request should be denied so we can get this case out of the way and move on to other things."

"Your Honor, with all due respect, I just finished pouring my heart out to this court, explaining that I have a female witness who could prove my client's innocence, but she's missing, so it would be impossible for me to proceed and zealously represent my client or his best interest without first locating my witness," he pleaded.

"Your Honor, this man does not care about the best interest of his client, nor does he show any respect for this court. He's been living and surviving off the reputation of his father and grandfather, and he mistakenly believes he'll be able to ride their coattails forever!" the district attorney said angrily.

Billy was completely shocked by the district attorney's statement. He stalled for a bit as he struggled to maintain professionalism—he could literally feel the anger inside of him begin to boil. "Your Honor, the last thing I need is to hear a remark like that from the district attorney. What he said was uncalled for. I don't understand where all of this animosity is coming from, but I do understand that he's way out of line for bringing my late father and grandfather into this."

The judge, along with many other spectators inside the crowded courtroom was stunned by the exchange of words between the two attorneys, Judge Oram was at a lost for words.

Prosecutor Philip Doolittle continued, "The mob doesn't run Las Vegas anymore. Mr. Brocks cannot expect for things to go his way every time he makes a request to this court, unless he's paid the judge off or some other government official like his father and grandfather used to do!" he stated boldly.

Billy became so enraged by the comment that he ran over and began punching the older man in the face repeatedly until the bailiff and other defense attorneys came over and pulled him off. Billy hadn't realized what he'd done until after it was over with.

"Order in this court!" The judge yelled while slamming his gavel repeatedly. "ORDER IN THE COURT!" he repeated.

The entire courtroom went into pandemonium after witnessing what happened. They were all scrambling around, trying to make sense of the attorneys unexpected quarrel, no one would have ever guessed an episode like this would take place inside a court of law. Meanwhile, the district attorney's face was a bloody mess as it swelled to nearly twice its normal size while several people gathered around him, helping him up from the floor. The bailiff asked that someone call 911 to get the shamed district attorney the medical help he desperately needed. The courtroom was immediately cleared except for the judge, the bailiff, and the young criminal defense attorney who was very uncomfortable after being sat down on a chair with a set of cold, hard handcuffs clamped tightly on his wrists. Judge Oram stared directly at Billy as he scolded him in the presence of the bailiff. He reminded him that he had taken an oath to practice law in a professional manner—an oath of which had just been violated. The judge also made comments despising the defense attorney for his unethical conduct and spoke very harshly before charging him with contempt of court. He expressed that he personally felt Billy should be disbarred for such behavior, but luckily the decision was not his to make. It would be up to the Las Vegas Bar Association to make that decision.

Judge Oram instructed his bailiff to place Billy inside one of the courts holding cells, and he was not to be let out until he authorized it. He added that he wanted the brazen defense lawyer to think long and hard about what he'd done while he try to decide what to do about punishment.

Billy Brocks did exactly that. He still couldn't believe what he'd done or how he had allowed himself to become so infuriated, the only thing he could do was think long and hard. He'd chosen a profession to help other people out of trouble, but now found himself in jail with no one who could let him out except for the man who'd just put him there. Billy had all sorts of questions going through his mind. He'd never been out of control like that before and had been surprised by his own actions. He had never even had a real fistfight before, so he cracked a smile as he realized that he'd actually won one.

At four o'clock that evening, Billy was finally released from his holding cell. The bailiff apologized for keeping him in so long but explained that Judge Oram had just given him authorization. He'd calmed down tremendously after spending six hours inside the lonely, cold holding cell, but he tried showing compassion after hearing from the bailiff that the district attorney had suffered a broken nose and a fractured jaw. He was in awe as he listened to the condition of Philip Doolittle, and his heart suddenly sank when the bailiff informed him that the man had promised to press charges. Billy stopped immediately in his tracks—he couldn't believe it.

At thirty-four years old and one of the most prominent defense lawyers in Las Vegas, he didn't know what the future held for him. His conduct had violated every rule that the Bar Association stood for, and he wasn't sure if he'd still be permitted to practice law with criminal charges pending against him. It had simply become too much drama for one day, and he thought he should spend some time sitting back to sort through it all.

He climbed inside his BMW and called Brocks & Brocks Law Offices from his cell phone. He tried to explain to his secretary Simone, what happened, but she stopped him as soon as he'd begun and told him she already knew about it. He wasn't aware that the entire incident had been plastered on the afternoon news a few hours after it happened. Every lawyer in town had been talking about it because most have been jealous of Billy ever since he'd started practicing law. Most felt like they had to work twice as hard to make a name for themselves, but Billy Brocks had been introduced to the practice with a silver spoon in his mouth since his father and grandfather were both well-known attorneys themselves. Billy's name alone had been opening doors for him, and he usually got all the best clients over all the other well-known attorneys. They felt that Billy's name had been working for him even when he did no work himself. Billy realized that a lot of people hated him just because he's the son and grandson of the father-son duo, Edwin Brocks, Sr., and Edwin Brocks, Jr. He now understood where the district attorney's animosity had stemmed from, so he placed the blame on his family's name for his current predicament.

After all, it was the two men's past that everyone really hated. He had no clue what their past were but he knew that whatever it was, it had come back to haunt him. Both men had long been dead, so everyone seemed to be taking their frustrations out on him. The young attorney with an impeccable reputation was now in trouble with the law himself, and was worried because his future as a licensed attorney was now in jeopardy.

About The Author

Truth Publications LLC founder, CEO and author Terrence Brothers has been turning the impossible into reality from behind bars. He's a different kind of inmate—a dreamer—one who looks to inspire—staying hopeful, refusing to give up despite the circumstances. Terrence's outside-the-box way of thinking has him wanting to do even bigger things. He's now writing screenplays for all of his novels.

Hollywood should pay closer attention to writers like him, especially those producers and directors who claims to keep it real.

If you'd like to contact this author directly, do so at:

Terrence Brothers #43397

P.O. Box 7007

Carson City, NV 89702

www.ingramcontent.com/pod-product-compliance
Lightning Source LLC
Chambersburg PA
CBHW031302170626
46807CB00001B/265